Distorted D

by

Louise Worthington

Also by Louise Worthington

Rachel's Garden of Rooms

Willow Weeps

Rosie Shadow

The Entrepreneur

For my husband, Nigel, and eldest sister, Sally, with love.

Chapter One

Lisa opens the front door in a dressing gown. Silky smooth, straight out of a B-movie. A pink-lipstick mouth opens but there's no sound. Bizarre ventriloquism happens when, from someplace inside the house, John's horrible omnipresent voice says, 'Who is it, love?'

Doris hasn't run for years. Never athletic, even as a child. The sight of her best friend's bare feet follows her home to 42 Utkinton Street, to her and John's home.

Inside, she's surprised there aren't dust sheets on the furniture. The clock on the mantelpiece ticks a hollow sound, so she vengefully removes the battery from its insides. Disembowelling it gives her a strange pleasure, but time hasn't stopped soon enough for the empty oven, which she'd switched on hours ago. It has cut out but it's warmed the kitchen up nicely.

She chooses red first, then rosé, then white. She likes the little clouds the red and rosé leave in the glass, streaking the colour a little.

It feels like there should be damp, dirty patches on the wall where stuff like fridges and wardrobes used to be. It annoys her that the furniture is in the same place as if nothing has happened, so she drinks in the bathroom. Sits on the lid of the toilet seat.

Downstairs, John's Christmas present stays unopened beneath the artificial Christmas tree – one they bought in B&Q in a January sale early on in their marriage. Every year John said the tree didn't owe them anything. Her present is just a small box wrapped up nicely because what matters is inside on a cream piece of card which tells him: *We're expecting a baby girl.*

As she listens to herself piss, she sees there's only one toothbrush in the pot by the sink. She thinks she hears a weight on the stairs, a hand turning a door handle, but there isn't. There's only Doris. Doormat Doris. The chanting continues in her head over and over. Through onion tears, she remembers through a gauze sentences, words, promises, as insignificant as the shopping lists and till receipts for the presents in her handbag, the food, the wine she's bought to celebrate the Christmas period. Doormat.

Her voice has walked out and left her too; carried itself down the stairs to someplace else where it might be listened to. 'Your fucking wife! That's who it is, *love.*' That's what she should have said to John, but she's never been good at thinking of a comeback on the spot. Besides, she has no courage to fight back, to admonish, because she is a damp firework.

If she could speak to them, she would say they have exploded her heart, released firecrackers through her senses. She wishes she could call the police, the ambulance, the fire brigade, to arrest and anaesthetise and waterboard the bastards.

If she screws up one eye, she can see the colour of the glass rolling pin on the bathroom tiles. It's a noisy one because it was expensive, carefully chosen by Doormat with the aid of an assistant in Tesco called Freda who had a nasty twitch in one eye. Freda's twitch got excited when Doris loaded her shopping trolley with twelve bottles of wine, four colours of each hue. She and John used to go on alcohol percentage and special offers but Freda opened her eyes to the aromas and blends and whatnot.

They make her drink. Guzzle until her stomach is a well, so full it begins to pour over the top and trickle down Utkinton Street, a red rivulet, an S shape all the way to the corner shop and back. They still make her drink, sip it if she has to, faces at the bottom of the glass. She keeps drinking, swaying, and they are still watching. Then it is dark, the colour of a drinker's liver.

This hurt is like a lit cigarette dabbed across the ribs. A grenade in her chest. Cock John and Twat Lisa stir cocktails with the linchpin. She breathes air through a damp handkerchief. Delirious, she lies on the cold tiles; sleep wants to take her.

As her mind swims in and out of consciousness, she sees herself driving, rain glistening on the road and smearing the windscreen. She swerves to miss a cat. John is a backseat driver, throwing commands out of his loose mouth, and Lisa's bound hand and foot in the back of the van with the paintbrushes he's left there after a job. She imagines herself driving to the middle of nowhere. No other cars and no other sound except John asking, asking, 'Where are we? Why are we here? Where are we going?' No one can see them for miles and miles.

The telephone rings in the downstairs kitchen. Doris washes her face in the sink, a vial for her tears. The sound of the water splashing on her skin takes her back to the trip the three of them took to Abersoch beach just a week ago, to the ancient cry of gulls above and their secret white bodies playing tunes in the churlish sky.

***

They stopped for a packed lunch in a layby just outside Bala. A wedge of cheese, Branston pickle and salad cream, just as John liked. He was wearing one of his best shirts, which fit his once rugby-playing physique rather well. Lately, even on weekends, he has liked to wear a shirt.

The three-hour journey to Abersoch in John's van was worth it when they saw the sea open its arms out wide, without limits. John accelerated at the vision and they let out a loud yell of excitement. Then the road shouted 'ARAF' so he did, and Doris was glad because she was carsick by then and he'd taken the last bend like he was on a racetrack. She'd opened the window and rain gently touched her bare arm like the caress of thin lips.

They could see the sea out of almost every window in the caravan, like a gallery of watercolours. Doris had packed three bags: one for John, one for herself and one for food. Lisa, tottering on her high heels, carried in a sage-green suitcase. Doris hoped she wouldn't be wearing them for the whole holiday, tapping away on the floor like a typist with a deadline when they should be relaxing, switching off from all that.

The walls were thin; they could hear John emptying the bagpipe of his bladder. They shared a look.

'The fish and chips are bound to be good here,' Lisa said from her bedroom with the door wide open. Doris caught a glimpse of her stuffing something black into the top drawer; it must have been underwear because Lisa only wears green or taupe clothes. Gold on very special occasions.

'Let's get some for supper,' John said from the bathroom, then he started singing 'The Reasons I Love You'.

John and Doris were in the largest bedroom because they'd paid for the caravan for a long weekend, then invited Lisa last minute because John said she'd pay for the petrol. Although Doris knew the caravan didn't cost much because it was out of season, she liked Lisa so she didn't grumble. Lisa didn't like sleeping in a bunk bed so she chose the other double room. Doris smiled privately: if she weren't with John, she'd have slept on the top bunk and wished Lisa was on the bottom one.

On the beach, John rolled up his trousers for a dip in the sea, exposing his tender white skin marbled with blue veins, which surprised Doris because he was normally shy about his body. The wind played with the sea, and black slimy seaweed was spewed on the beach as if the sea had eaten too much of it.

Lisa looked for shells and pebbles, then wrote her name in the sand in capital letters, except for the 'i' which was lower case and had a love heart for a dot. Doris watched the clouds move. She would have been happy to stay on the beach and make an omelette later for everyone but John and Lisa had fish and chips on their mind and, even if there had been a vote, she would have been in the minority. That's how it was for her.

John said he was too tired to drive and, because Lisa had hurt the back of her leg doing a yoga pose, Doris was pushed into taking her first driving lesson. Lisa had taken up yoga after her mum passed away. The strain was caused by a cat- or dog-related pose, or something related to an animal – she couldn't remember which. John said he knew a good physio who could sort it out, and laughed like a hyena.

There was a strange smell coming from the engine of the van as Doris drove down a one-way street. 'You need to change gear,' he sniggered, like she was a fool.

Doris fumbled the van into a parking space behind a pub. It was painted a sickly yellow hue. From inside the van, she watched John and Lisa chat and gesture. Her legs had turned to jelly from the drive.

'Two for one on them, love,' an assistant said, wearing a necklace of yellow-and-white beads that reminded Doris of daisies in her mother's back garden.

The traditional sea-side shop sold buckets and spades, surfboards and postcards displayed in holders that made circles on the spot. The blackboard by the door used to say *10% off Snorkels*, but it looked like *Skol* now, which made John laugh. There was a small yellow spade just right for a child's hand that asked to be picked up. Doris hurriedly put it back, bought a postcard instead – one of the beaches in Abersoch – except the sea shimmered like it was wearing a diamanté dress.

After supper, John wanted a couple of pints in the pub while Lisa and Doris spent a few quid on the arcade machines. Lisa jiggled around to a song someone kept paying for on the juke box. Over and over. Doris never thought for one moment who might be placing their coins in the slot. She started drinking pineapple juice because she was full of gas after all the Coke she'd drunk at the start of the evening. John said she needed the practice, so she'd be driving back to the caravan.

There was a tear in one eye and the smell of white wine on Lisa's breath when she confessed how aggrieved she'd been by her mother's will, which left half of the house to her brother Steve, who hadn't seen his mother in years – years! Oh, the injustice and the betrayal after all that she'd sacrificed for her mother and all that John had done to decorate the house and repair the washing machine and the tumble dryer. She said this was her first holiday in years. After giving her mother bed baths for longer than she cared to remember, Lisa said that the day she passed away was the best and worst day of her life. John and Doris listened like the best counsellors in town. It was late by the time they got back to the caravan and then John was asleep as soon as his head hit the pillow.

'John said I drove home like a dream, bless him. It's not often he compliments me. Night, Lisa.'

Doris was going to tell him about the baby – their first – it being such a romantic spot overlooking the sea, with the stars and a full silver moon, and it being their wedding anniversary. She was going to ask him to walk with her, take a short stroll down to the beach, just the two of them, dip their toes in the water. And then she was going to tell him. He was bound to ask her if she was sure, and she was. A scan showed their little kidney bean. Not even Lisa knew.

John snored – he always did after a lot of ale, so Doris crept into the spare room, climbed onto the top bunk. Next door, Lisa was awake; Doris heard her tapping on her phone. The rain started gently at first then it hammered and rebounded, grazing and bruising the tin roof, making it cry out in metallic-sounding pain. Doris listened hard for a while, wondering if the fish in the sea knew it was raining or were oblivious to what was going on above the line of the sea and sky.

Her bed was warmer now; she felt happy and safe in the warmth, listening to the rain and the wind, with their baby growing inside her. She imagined a skylight for their child so she could see the moon and the stars.

Lisa must have been asleep because the tension had gone out from under the roof. If Lisa were outside in the wind and rain, her unruly red hair would have expanded and ruffled like feathers.

Before breakfast, they walked along the beach. Lisa's name had vanished so she wrote it again. She said the sea looked grey and empty without sailing boats or swimmers. John offered to get in for a swim but she touched him on the arm and said there was no need. He thought the sea looked ravenous, like it wanted to devour anything in its way. Nobody asked what Doris saw in the sea. Now she'd say a mirror.

When they got back to 42 Utkinton Street, the house was cold and damp. John talked about foreign countries – Greece, Spain, Ibiza – where the temperature was so hot you could sit outside in nothing but a T-shirt all night long. He talked about hotels with all-inclusive deals that she'd never heard of before. It was all foreign.

The next morning, Doris was up early. She had the radio on – Christmas songs – while she was washing up. The presenter said snow was forecast for Christmas Eve from around lunchtime. How perfect. But then she heard the front door close.

'John?' she called, then watched him hop in his van, a bag slung on the passenger seat.

***

Doris wakes up on the bathroom floor; the tiles swim around, so they look prettier than they are. She strokes the wall; it glows with cold. A cluster of toenails and fingernails peek-a-boo behind the toilet, and the scum of congealed skin, hair and snot hide behind the sink. Skin: it's just epidermis and dermis. Did John and Lisa make love in this house? In the caravan? The precision and predictability of the tiles on the floor insult her colliding emotion.

Doris uses the basin to haul her sandbag body up from the bathroom floor, checks she still has a reflection in the mirror. She sits on the toilet with her head in her hands, grime clinging to her clothes and hair, her socks red from the blood and the red wine. Less than a week ago they were in Abersoch together.

***

Time put on a pair of stilettos then to walk around the house slowly and noisily, hour after hour. Perhaps he'd gone to collect a Christmas present for her? A last-minute purchase? She didn't think to put on the heating just for one. The lounge flickered green and orange from the television hour after hour. The smudgy orange streetlight kept her company through till morning. She tried each seat in the lounge. Much later, she remembered to eat and smiled at the light that popped into the kitchen when the fridge door opened. The turkey was in there, a drawer full of vegetables. Her stomach clenched. She switched on the oven but it didn't work. The morning brought light at least, but nothing else.

The telephone rang but she didn't answer. The message was from Lisa: 'Sorry.'

Lisa must have been cut off. Doris listened to the message again but it didn't make sense. Worried something might be wrong, she called back. There was no answer, so she walked round to Lisa's house wrapped in her favourite yellow scarf.

The streets were deserted. Doris tried not to look into people's houses but so many had gathered around a table by a window that it was hard not to look in. She watched a red-and-gold cracker pulled in two. Did it make a sound?

If only the roof of the caravan had lifted off like a giant's hand opening a tin. The sea and the wind could have poured inside and peered at the three of them in their beds like dolls in a dolls' house – but the dolls were in the wrong beds. Only the stars stare at the bruises on Doris's chest and the hollowed-out body like an avocado without a stone.

John never opened his present, which was just as well because later she found herself on the bathroom floor beside smashed wine bottles and the putrid wine and acid she'd vomited from the very depths of her stomach. Even the tiles in the bathroom were tainted pink; the whole room was like a medieval operating theatre, a bloody chamber, red and rosé ricocheted and pin-balled until the internal explosion, the final unscrewing of a screw top, pop of a cork. Their baby.

***

She blinks her eyes at the stinging sensation in her mind and body. This time her name is written in the sand with diamonds and gems. She sees her name on a kite flying in the blue sky. She sees John and Lisa walking hand and hand towards the sea and it grabs their ankles, it drags them to their deaths, quietly and purposefully. She wishes she were a fish so she could watch their muddy mouths opening and closing in the green sea, the silt landing on their eyelids, their last words … sorry. Sorry.

Sick of the sight of her vomit on the bathroom tiles, Doris staggers into the bedroom. She tosses and turns, hour after hour; the memories of John and Lisa and her grow thistles, nestled in overgrown grass threaded with weeds, poisonous wildflowers, leaves throbbing with blood-red veins. The photo album of all her lovely fake memories won't shut. She pleads for a zip to the album, a fusion.

A local paper is pushed through the letterbox. Doris puts it straight in the bin because she is no longer connected with this town, this county or country. This planet. This universe.

Chapter Two

Is she dead skin to them?

Doris spends Christmas Day cleaning the house, starting with the bathroom because she's fixated with the idea of dead skin, the flakes of epidermis and dermis, and the stray hairs from John's full head of hair. Lisa has bouncy, curled hair the colour of temptation. Attempting to erase their footprints in the house takes most of the day. The skin on her hands becomes dry and cracked from the cleaning agents and the water, but at least the falling flakes are from her own skin.

The sun eventually punches a hole through the opaque sky and shines on the view from the window in the lounge: a dividing road edged by pavement, red-brick terraces, mirror images of her marital home. She wonders if others can still see number 42 or whether a giant eraser has rubbed it out and everything inside it, including her, except for a neon sign shouting *NAÏVE. FOOL.* She couldn't possibly set foot outside now: she would be like the emperor in his new clothes. Did Cock and Twat laugh at her all the while?

By four o'clock she's made a funeral pyre of the detritus of their marriage, including pictures of Cock and Twat from a montage of photographs that used to hang in the downstairs loo: so many smiles in so many locations, the three of them, the pair of conspirators right in front of her each and every day as she took a pee.

Ugly thoughts start popping into her head at alarming speed. Were they seeing each other when they went to Bath that time to watch the rugby? Did they have secret kisses when her back was turned in Liverpool at the Albert Dock? Gullible, unsuspecting Doris, all the while her thinking Twat was such a sweet friend to join in with their trips. It never occurred to her to question why it took her husband such a long time to come home after he walked Twat back to her place after a day out or a few drinks at the pub. Never. Or why he could see to the decorating and the jobs at her house but not their own.

If she'd seen it coming, it might not have hurt so much. But the sting of that slap, the shudder from the unexpected sound, it sent her reeling. Worse than that, it made her question everything she had known about him, her best friend and herself. What or who could she trust? The feeling of betrayal, the double-shot, the double-whammy, the Go Large, the dual-approach to devastation, it certainly hit the spot. Husband and friend. Did betrayal get any bigger? Louder?

She finds a small box of matches in the kitchen drawer; she only needs one match because the funeral pyre is flammable with the fake tree and Cock's Christmas present to get it going nicely. Columns of smoke rise from the modest back yard, a taste like locusts spreading out over all the other back yards in this unfashionable part of Shrewsbury.

She tosses in the turkey and veg. Luckily it is late December: too cold to dry the washing. She has forgotten it's Christmas Day when few people would be washing and drying their clothes even in the brightest of sun. She watches the flames and the long sighs of smoke, and she wishes for crackling flames to reach inside their nostrils, brains, to singe her innocent name there forever with a pure blue flame.

Is she so difficult to talk to? After eleven years of marriage, why couldn't John show her the courtesy of explaining why he was leaving her? To just close the door. She shakes her head at the memory of the sound, the emptiness of the hall, then the answer found through the window and later confirmed at Lisa's front door.

Once the bonfire has burnt itself into a smouldering pile of red and grey ashes, Doris pokes at the debris with the pointy end of a wedding umbrella, turns over the charred fragments of her past, like she is burying herself alive. She replaces the montage of photographs with a mirror so she can look at herself while she is on the loo to check she still has a reflection and to see if she can like herself a little bit.

She wishes her knuckles were blue and swollen from punching her cheating husband on his arse and slapping Twat hard across that tasty face of hers. She imagines herself pushing Cock's flabby legs akimbo in a pair of stilettos bought especially for the occasion, like a switchblade, kicking him square between the legs, with Lisa watching on with a cheek full of fire. She imagines sound coming from his cheating mouth like curlicues of smoke – a chalk outline of his body on Twat's carpet.

Having forgotten to eat, her energy is fading now. The darkness outside is a relief. The last thing she does before bed is to arrange objects on the window-ledge in the lounge so passers-by can enjoy them in the morning: a postcard of Abersoch beach; an avocado stone; a box of matches, and the slop and stink from the bathroom floor in a plastic tub Cock had once eaten his favourite vanilla ice-cream from. It is her post to the outside world, her own kind of oversharing. Who else is there to talk to? Not her mother. Never.

It is a relief when she sleeps so she can stop being her conscious self for a while. Get a rest from being useless and inhabiting the frightened place she's become.

By Boxing Day, she stops consciously waiting. She spends the day reading in the lounge, occasionally looking up through the window to catch a glimpse of a ribbon in a child's hair, the paperboy with his luminous bag, the ones who walk, hold hands and laugh and don't know anything. For a moment she thinks she sees Lisa's red hair, her bouncing curls, but if it is Lisa she doesn't stop.

The bathroom is a room Doris finds herself avoiding as much as possible. No amount of scrubbing the floor can erase the memory of losing her daughter in there, where a horrible nameless baptism of kinds took place.

The buzz of a scooter wakes Doris up to an insatiable hunger which she satisfies with trifle, Quality Streets and ice cream. The telephone rings. She knows it's Mother but she has nothing to say to her, to anyone. Silence has grown around her like a cocoon.

For the next week, flotsam from the outside world – a window cleaner looking for work, local newspapers, junk mail – reminds her of how frightening and thrusting the world outside is. The front door rubs up against the street. Sometimes she hears footsteps so close to the door her heartbeat becomes irregular. Life outside is busy now it's the end of the holidays and folk are full of renewed purpose, New Year resolutions.

She trudges from one end of the day to the next until she opens a book and disappears inside. After the fifth Jenga-style coffee table of books, she sees she needs a place to go. The lounge may cope with another two tables – which she calculates to be around twenty books – but that's only about another month of escapism.

11

The school holidays are about to end; the thought of returning to work as a teaching assistant in a primary school makes her stomach clench. She couldn't even face her favourite pupil, Izzy with a gap in her front tooth through which she likes to insert her tongue when she's thinking. She can hear Izzy chattering about the visit from Father Christmas and Rudolf.

Will John be working now? How will Lisa spend her days? They have a new routine to establish now they're living together. Lisa won't know how he likes his eggs in the morning. With spit and shell.

***

A watercolour memory invades Doris's space, of her and John lying on the grass in Grosvenor Park in Chester. It was the beginning of summer, there were roses with pink velvet petals and purple delphiniums in the borders, and he'd said her purple dress was the same colour. She was pleased he'd noticed her dress because it was new, a colour she thought suited her. Even though she hadn't had a drink, she felt attractive. John was a bear of a man even then, liked his food. When he'd rummaged in the tote bag they'd packed, she'd thought it was for a sandwich or a packet of crisps but it wasn't. It was for an engagement ring.

They got married in a registry office at Gretna Green, close to where her mother lived. John's mother had passed away. She'd called herself a clairvoyant but she hadn't seen the Grim Reaper coming. So, it was just his dad, just the four of them.

Doris had hired a beautiful satin wedding dress embellished with beads, and carefully chosen shoes the colour and gloss of deep-sea pearls. They were more of a slipper with a small heel, which made her feet look long and thin. A Cinderella-kind of shoe, but she planned on keeping the pair forever. Until the funeral pyre.

She'd not seen her father for more than twenty years and hadn't thought of him that much, but she did that day. John's dad gave her away, a sickly sort of man with watery blue eyes. His wedding present was a fireguard, an odd sort of present for a childless couple, but it gave him an excuse to talk about 'their palace', which he'd gifted to his son before moving into sheltered accommodation. It had burnt very nicely with the fake Christmas tree. Though she didn't like the phrase

12

'give her away', she understood its significance and was only too happy to take John's paw.

From Gretna Green, the newlyweds drove into Scotland for a weekend in Edinburgh with a casserole dish in the boot – her mother's wedding present. Between changing gear, John held her hand, occasionally tapping the wedding ring on the gear stick to a tune in his head. It was spring and Doris was thirty-four.

John said he thought Arthur's Seat rose up like a giant from the car park where they ate cheese-and-pickle sandwiches and drank lemonade. A falconer was giving a demonstration at the foot of the hill, which John watched in awe, but Doris turned her back when the falcon took flight only to swoop back and land on the man's glove, jangling the bell on its jesses.

They didn't hike to the top of Arthur's Seat, just skirted around the foot of the hill then used the public toilets. Doris remembers the white buddleia that grew through the cracks in the pavement; its tenacious beauty lured white butterflies to its delicate colour. From there they drove into the city centre where they checked into a guest house and Doris wrote in the visitors' book using her new surname. Gambol.

***

By the second week in January Doris is an accomplished internet shopper with a knack for finding bargain books, discounted food and wine. The web is a kidney-dialysis machine working 24/7. She likes to hold the hand of the mouse and move it to the right spot. Click, and it is all hers. After the doctor had signed her off work, she'd celebrated by buying an Alexa voice-controlled speaker, so now she has someone to talk to and a voice to read audiobooks to her when her eyes get tired. It is an ugly automated voice but at least it is female. There is no need to leave the house ever again.

The memories of her marriage are like silt at the bottom of a water trough, stirred up by John's departure to be with Lisa, turning them a murky green. If only it were just a matter of taking a tea-strainer to the silt.

She's noticed how her hearing is more acute to the kitchen tap, the surge of the boiler as the pilot light flicks on, the creak of the second stair, the shuffle of post landing on the floor in the hall. She hears these sounds and more – except the opening of the front door, the rustle of John hanging his coat on the hall peg, or the sound of him calling her name. She orders an electric toothbrush which arrives within twenty-four hours, just for a different sound. Then pikelets because she and John used to love crumpets on a wet Sunday afternoon, with plenty of raspberry jam and tea. She collects corks and screw tops to replace her old memories and makes patterns with them on the kitchen window ledge.

Chapter Three

If it wasn't for a hacking cough, she might not have spoken to anyone for years. But the cough gets so bad that her neighbour on the right calls round. The finger is on her doorbell for so long that Doris knows she has no choice but to answer it. Whoever it is wants to see her.

'Sorry to bother you, love. I live next door. Tina.'

Tina looks faintly amusing in her onesie. The crease on Doris's forehead forms because she can't decide if the woman is a cow or a zebra. A cow. Doris's mouth splutters into life with a long, dry cough that sends her face tomato-red. The coughing goes on for several minutes.

'It's that, you see. You're ill. I'm next door and I hear you, cough, cough, cough, all through the night. It's been going on for weeks and, well – to be honest, babe, I need a decent night's sleep. Have you seen a doctor?'

Doris shakes her head, afraid to speak, unsure what she'll sound like having only spoken to Alexa who isn't sensitive to her tone of voice. Many a time Doris has wished she could pick up on sarcasm.

'You don't look well. Do you need me to get a doctor over?' Tina peers inside the dim, narrow hall and raises her eyebrows at the state of the wallpaper and the threadbare carpet. 'Look, is your husband not around?'

'Cock's run off with Twat!' Doris yells, her fists clenched, knuckles blanched. Surprisingly, her voice works fine. A little rough around the edges but clear enough.

Tina looks quite impressed by her choice of vocabulary and concision. 'You poor thing. I'm going to get my keys and then drive you round to the doctor's. Be back in a jiffy.'

And she is.

The combination of Tina in a cow onesie and the pitiful sound of Doris's cough give the doctor's receptionist no hesitation in squeezing in an appointment with Dr Timpson. Each thought they got the appointment because of the sight or sound of the other. Tina disappears outside the surgery for a fag as Doris hovers in the waiting room for a short while, embarrassed to be the centre of attention. The plastic chairs line the walls of the square room making eye contact with other patients difficult to avoid. The seating arrangement gives the place a feeling of a village hall without the community cheer.

Apart from the mirror in the loo that only reflects her face, Doris hasn't looked at her whole self for some time. There hasn't been any real need to with staying indoors all the time and besides, part of her worried that from the waist down she's shrivelled up now that her womb is defunct. To keep down on the washing, she's been wearing and sleeping in the same clothes for quite a while. And bathing hasn't been a priority either, because it involves going into the bathroom. It all seems like too much effort. Her face is clean and she smooths her hair down each morning with a splash of cold water. The top bit of her is fine, she thinks. But Dr Timpson says otherwise.

By the time Doris leaves his consulting room, there is a waiting room full of bad-tempered ill people. Bodies have arranged themselves at all angles in the uncomfortable chairs.

After her spate of silence, Doris found she couldn't stop talking once she started. Dr Timpson is such an excellent listener. At the end of her monologue he smiled at her warmly and said she was depressed. He explained that depression is a mental illness which needs treatment, just like a physical illness – a broken arm or a gammy toe. It isn't always known how long it can take to feel better, but he repeated over and over 'it will get better'. She thinks he is an amazing doctor to be able to see inside her head and to know it will heal up nicely. It is such a relief.

Scared to stay in the vicinity of angry, ill people, as soon as she's collected her prescription she heads for the door to find Tina. Her yellow Beetle is still there, but no Tina. Doris follows her nose to the back of the building to find Tina on her tenth cigarette, stomping up and down in a decidedly un-cow like way.

'You took your bloody time! Bloody hell, you owe me a packet of fags!'

Doris smiles. The first one in a long time. She waves the paper bag of drugs like a robber's stash of loot.

16

'Blimey! You look like a different woman already!' Tina narrows her eyes. 'Have you had sex in there? You could have got me. I've got cobwebs down there!'

The laughter brings on a coughing fit but Doris feels better than she has in a long time. By the time Tina has driven them home, Doris has learned a lot about the ups and downs of being a hairdresser and the merits of owning a pet over keeping a man. Tina's menagerie includes a tortoise, a hamster and a cat that likes to sleep on its back, choices in part determined by the animals' ability to cope with long periods of absence, as Tina likes to go to concerts whenever she can afford it. Farmer Phil's festival especially. The daisy on the dashboard bobs its innocent head merrily in tune with a band called The Falling Skies.

'I love your car,' Doris says. 'It's my favourite colour.'

The coughing doesn't subside straight away so Doris sleeps on the sofa, the furthest thing away from Tina's house on the right.

She duly drops round two packets of cigarettes to Tina's house after ordering them on the internet while enjoying the irony of a present that has all the makings of giving Tina a bad cough. Dr Timpson said it would take a few weeks for the antidepressants to work and the cough would subside after a course of antibiotics.

Doris is speaking again. It is a small victory for the face in the downstairs loo mirror. And she's made a friend. Her mother is relieved she has medication and a friend, probably because otherwise she'd feared a visit might be needed.

Doris's forehead rumples at the sound of the doorbell at 9.30 on a Wednesday morning. The door opens onto a woman shaped like an iceberg. Her diminutive upper body appears to have been stuck on the lower body of a much larger person. Any profession or business could don the suit and the briefcase, but the glossy brochure headed *Town and Country* tells Doris everything she needs to know about this iceberg. The second she sees the brochure is the second someone gets hold of that elastic slice of time and stretches it – pulls it so hard that it goes on and on and on until she lets go.

'Cock sent you!' Doris blurts out, her face scarlet with anger, the volume disproportionately loud to the proximity of the woman.

Doris is aware of the flicker of fear across the woman's face and the interrupted footsteps of a couple on the opposite side of the

17

pavement. A couple she knows moved into number 30 not that long ago. Once she would have been happy for them, waved, even chatted on a chipper day. They move on despite seeing the distress and emotion on Doris's face. The man takes the woman's hand in his in a reassuring gesture that says their world is sane.

Doris sighs and says in a resigned voice, 'You'd better come in, I suppose.'

'Mrs Gambol—'

'My name is Doris. Come in before anyone else sees.'

They sit face to face at the kitchen table. A passer-by might be forgiven for thinking a competitive game of chess is about to commence. Doris doesn't offer tea, even though her manners make her feel a little guilty. The woman's name is Megan and she's a senior consultant from Town and Country instructed by John Gambol to sell his house. He'd assured Megan that Doris was expecting her to call round to value the house and she would cooperate during the viewing and selling process.

'Cock is a liar and a low-life. He makes Fagin look honest.'

'Mr Gambol tells me you're separated and he owns this house. Once his father's, I believe. Is that correct?'

Doris's nod is like Izzy's nod when she knows she's done something wrong, like stealing someone's pen or pushing an irritable boy over in the playground. Did you do it? Nod.

'He's provided me with a copy of the prenuptial agreement you signed to confirm this.' She pushes a copy under Doris's nose. 'He wants the house to go on the market now, as the spring and summer are the best times to sell.' She waits for the look of horror on Doris's face to fade a little. 'I am sorry.' She looks around the kitchen with an appraising eye. 'I would have phoned first only—'

Doris suddenly stands up, sending the chair screeching on the tiled floor. She can't find the words. She wants to crawl under the stairs and close the cupboard door behind her, a place small and dark. If she had the courage, she'd run out of the door. 'Get on with it then. I don't have a choice, do I?'

'I'll leave you with this brochure and our terms and conditions. Thank you.'

18

'How long?' Doris asks, her hands on the back of kitchen chair clenched so tightly her knuckles are beginning to hurt.

'Ten minutes.'

'Till I have to move out.'

'At least ten weeks, or longer. It depends on how quickly it sells. Mr Gambol will move back in in the autumn if it doesn't sell for the asking price.'

'I've lived here all my married life. Eleven years. It was our wedding anniversary in December.'

'I'm sorry.' Megan looks away, embarrassed, and leaves a business card on the brochure.

'He left me for my best friend, you know.'

It isn't the first time a stranger has unburdened herself to Megan. It happened once for a full fifteen minutes on the train from Telford to Shrewsbury. A person can say a lot in that time. 'This must be very difficult for you.' She casts her eye over the brochure, rearranges her jacket. 'Town and Country have experience in handling difficult situations. I promise I won't be here long.'

She is true to her word; the estate agent puts a value on Doris's home in less than ten minutes and thus begins her journey towards homelessness. Not a compliment or a considerate gesture, not really. Doris looks anxiously at the calendar on the wall, at the picture of a robin on a snow-covered bird table. The next page is a picture of a daffodil. She has a deadline. Her mother says deadlines are great for getting things done, otherwise, she'd never pay for her TV license.

The For Sale sign goes up a week later, right above the front door like a flag of surrender. If her neighbours haven't heard about the separation, they'll work it out now. Doris wouldn't have even known the sign was there if Tina hadn't called round, horrified. She'd left Doris's house even more horrified after learning the situation her friend finds herself in.

As gently as she knows how, Tina encourages Doris to go back to work or get a new job so she can afford to rent somewhere. The next day the job section of the local newspaper arrives through the letterbox with pink felt-tip pen on it. A few days after that, Doris receives a copy of the house particulars and a short note asking her to remove the objects from the lounge window and tidy up the place. She flushes her kidney bean down the loo while crying hysterically.

The last time she saw Dr Timpson he'd said much the same thing as Tina, but in his well-spoken, kindly efficient way; he'd said it was time for her to get a job, get out of the house, meet some people. Just hearing him list those three things made Doris feel anxious and exhausted, even in the blanched space of his consulting room with him looking at her with his caring face. It was clear that she had no choice, unless she slept in a doorway or returned to her mother's house. She considered both options with equal disdain. Neither was possible.

Chapter Four

Her heels click on the pavement like they are typing a letter to a stranger. She speed walks down Utkinton Road to the bus stop, where leaves and debris make shorthand squiggles on the pavement. Once she reaches the bus stop, she can lift her head and look around a little at the familiar scene from under the plastic awning. It seems a tsunami of litter has torn through the streets and rubbished her town. It seems the sun has been stolen and replaced with a fake gold coin. It seems like people are on speed. If an enormous skateboard arrives instead of the bus, it won't shake Doris any more than she already is. She is glad to find a book in her handbag to escape the world she lives in as she waits for the bus to arrive. She reads *The Scarlet Letter* with half her face buried in her yellow scarf for comfort.

There is a paragraph of litter by the bus stop which she reads with a frown: if it weren't for the interview, Doris would pick up the litter. She normally does. But her hands are clean; she has washed her hair and brushed it too. Best stay clean for the interview, she thinks. The thick black tights she is wearing appear to be slipping down her legs. She gives them an ungainly yank.

The single-decker bus – number 3 to Shrewsbury Town Centre – pulls up on time and whisks her away from Utkinton Street where terraced houses nestle on the gentle slope next to one another as if for company on a drunken night out. She smiles when they pass her terraced house: number 42 – bye-bye house. The familiar page of her street is turned over out of sight, making her heart jump like a frog touched by an electrode.

No one speaks on the bus and no eyes make contact, so her back finally makes contact with the back of the seat.

I'm Doris. Pleased to meet you.

She has rehearsed her opening lines in the belief that if she can deliver them she can make it through the interview. In her left hand she clutches the letter confirming the time, place and date of the interview. Two names: Colleen Collect and Matthew Morris, Darwin Library, Central Street, Shrewsbury.

Minutes away from her stop, Doris thinks she is shrinking. Has she mistakenly eaten a Mr Wonker treat on her journey instead of a Polo mint? Through the diminishing lens of her eye, Doris feels so small and insignificant she isn't sure she can get off the bus to reach the gap to the pavement. Has she turned into one of Kafka's insects? It isn't a story she particularly likes, but she had empathised with Gregor Samsa at that moment and it had got her through a very average Tuesday.

Hiss goes the door as it opens.

Doris decides that, even if she has metamorphosed and is minute, she can make a run for the door. If she's going to die, she'd rather die on the street than on a tatty, stale bus. So she picks up her feet and runs for it, down the aisle, through the door, onto the street. The bus driver looks askance at the figure on the pavement and makes a *What the fuck?* expression.

It's 9.35am: twenty-five minutes until the interview with Mr Morris and Mrs Collect. Before Cock royally fucked her over, Doris had been a frequent visitor to the Darwin library. Saturdays. She read the reading list for the local book club (posted on the notice board each month) but she didn't incline to talk with strangers about how she was moved by what she read, so she never actually attended. She has perfectly good conversations with herself about the interesting characters and settings. Book clubs are all a bit too up close and personal for her, like shaving her face for a TV advert, which she doesn't need to do. Thank you.

Once inside Darwin Library, Doris drops her shoulders. Quiet. Not silence but the gentle quiet of people in company, turning pages, browsing shelves, restraining their voices. Bliss. So many of her friends are here on the first floor, which is devoted to fiction: Rebecca; Dorian Gray; Hamlet; Jane Eyre, and Harold Fry. There is a sound of people thinking, a chuckle, a page-turning. A grey-haired gentleman in enormous spectacles relaxes in a soft chair, his legs elegantly crossed. He smiles at something he reads. A casually dressed young woman browses the romance section. She puts one hand on the spines as if she might feel the pulse of the chosen one.

In Darwin's library, Doris feels less alone than she has in a long time. It seems to her that there are hundreds of voices that want to talk to her. Some of them are a bit different, like her. Some voices have had their heart broken; some are warriors, philanthropists or trail-blazers and more – women she can only ever dream of being. There is so much chatter under that roof, but for once Doris doesn't mind the sound; they have something worth saying which doesn't hurt her ears.

'Excuse me, I'm here for an interview with Mr Morris and Mrs Collect,' she says at the central desk, glad the first pair of eyes looking at her quizzically belong to a slightly cross-eyed female wearing comically large beads. Above her head, the sign says, 'Check In' and to the left 'Check Out' like an airport terminal. 'Doris Gambol.'

Doris has never been upstairs in the library before, let alone up two flights of stairs. The place expands on itself like a robotic leg. The winding staircase within the blanched stone walls has an air of Rapunzel's tower. She diligently follows Big Beads, glad she doesn't have to climb stairs and make small talk at the same time.

She imagines what a Mrs Colleen Collect might look like. White teeth, a fresh smile. Probably middle to late middle age like her, except Colleen has a wedding ring. A shiny silver one probably. What might she collect? Sponges and toothpicks, Doris thinks. As for Mr Morris, she'd rather not imagine him at all, although a talking point could be the alliterative Mm sound of his name that once featured on a TV commercial for Bisto.

Desk. No window. Hot. The room couldn't be more uninviting.

'Do sit down, Ms Gambol. Thank you for coming. I'm Matthew Morris and this is Colleen Collect. I'm the manager of library services in Shropshire and Colleen is the chief librarian. We want to ask you a few questions about your application but, before we do, are there any questions you have for us? It only seems fair to me that you ask questions as well as us.' Mr Morris earnestly smiles a jolly smile.

Doris looks at the screen hanging from the wall like a telescreen from *1984*.

'I'm not Winston. I'm Doris.'

Mr Morris follows her gaze and laughs. 'Not a generous helping of books here. Can I have some more please?'

He chortles but hastily stops when Colleen gives him a quizzical stare. '*Oliver Twist*,' he explains. 'What do you think of the library here, Doris?'

'There's a lot of crime and not a lot of poetry or classic literature. It's rather like Stan's Supermarket – there's too much shelf-space given over to the same stuff on repeat but with different names and nuances. Why not have one or two really tasty fish cakes rather than a range of ones with some fish, no fish, great fish, like fish but not quite fish, fish of no origin, fish in a former life, aspiring fish? The best kind of marketing says it how it is. Honest synopses.'

'I see your point. What's the best kind of fish?'

'The fresh kind.'

'You will have seen in the letter we sent you that part of the interview process involves participation in one of our book clubs.'

'Yes, I've been rather dreading it.'

This time Colleen laughs. They are meeting in a small conference room just off the horror section. There is a lot of glass in the small conference room, a clumsy table and ten chairs that are somewhere between being comfortable and uncomfortable. The strip light is so stark it's accusatory, and the blinds across the ample windows sigh a lot. All in all, in Doris's humble opinion, it couldn't have been less conducive to a chat about a decent book.

Mr Morris and Mrs Collect ask her to sit down and wait for the group to arrive.

'What do you think of our book club room?' Mr Morris asks, while pulling his chair closer into the circle.

'It's more suited to a meeting about revising the packaging for Hobnobs or the target market for Dairy Lea than talking about a good book.'

He explodes with laughter. Colleen has never seen him so tickled. In a state bordering panic, Doris watches the small group shuffle into the room. She counts five faces plus the volunteer, Frederick. Six people in one room. Desk. Chairs. Strip light. Six. Panic is simmering until she sees the text on the table: *The Bloody Chamber.*

Doris can't help herself; she feels so impassioned it removes all traces of self-consciousness and fear. Angela Carter's words, not her own, save her; they get her the job, transport her from the Dairy Lea room into fairy tales of wolves, red chokers, gothic castles, and emancipated women. They all come to life in a triumphant struggle for freedom. Hurrah!

There is drizzle as she exits the bus and glances at the paragraph of litter she'd noted in the morning. It is nuzzled up against the far end of the bus stop, trapped by metal and concrete. The light in the bus station flickers on and off, on and off, as if it is scared of its purpose now it is dark. Cars speed by in a hurry for dinner, TV, bed. Doris is desperate for home too, but habits die hard.

She doesn't have a plastic bag with her, so she removes the bulky items from the pile of litter: a Pepsi bottle; a Carling can; Tesco's prawn sandwich, and a brown paper bag, perhaps once home to sausage rolls or a pasty like the ones John used to love. She takes these items home in her tote bag like abandoned kittens. Her hands feel grubby as she walks the last few meters before turning the key in the door and depositing the rescued items in her overflowing pedal bin.

When Tina asks her what the interview day was like, she can't remember a single word. It has been wiped, assuming it was ever stored. Perhaps it just blew through her memory, in and out of her ears with no rest in between. So, she tells Tina what she can, that she got the job.

Chapter Five

Colleen is methodical in inducting Doris into the library routines and policies. She explains that the ground floor houses much of the large print, audiobooks, computers and popular genres such as crime and romance, plus a discreet section on health. It meets the needs of the majority and the less mobile or claustrophobic – or those who prefer to avoid getting in a lift.

The second floor provides a home for meeting rooms and much of the non-fiction, art, music, sports and crafts. The doors to the third floor open automatically, initiating the electric lights. They switch themselves on along the ceiling like an upside-down runway.

February: the magnificent windows look out into semi-darkness as four o'clock approaches. Perhaps due to the size of the windows and the height of the gothic ceiling, it is cold on the top floor, so cold it feels like they could be outside. Of all the floors, it is generally the least used because many of the books are academic textbooks. There's also a section on poetry, literary criticism and plays.

The wheels of the trolley resist the carpet as Colleen pushes it out of the lift into the hall; they reverse themselves like a toddler dragging their heels, a 360-degrees U-turn. Undeterred, she pushes harder until a mouse squeak communicates their submission.

Colleen lowers her voice to a conspiratorial tone as they make their way down the central aisle where more and more books litter their path. Annoyed at the carelessness of people, Colleen tuts and bends down to pick several of them up.

Whoosh!!

Doris ducks as a book flies over her head, narrowly missing her eyebrow. Then another and another. Red volumes with a black spine.

PPSSSSSSSS!

From one side of the room to the other, books and words are flying, crashing, picking up speed between the shelves, dive-bombing to the ground only to catapult to the ceiling. Now there is a hailstorm, some big, some small, pelting from left to right. Colleen puts up her hand to deflect a large volume from hitting her face. A mouth is making sounds from somewhere out of sight. Colleen's head and neck look this way and that way like a curious hen. They hear a string of alliterative verbs and a train made of the alphabet.

Chooo! Chooo!

Doris gazes up at the ceiling with her mouth open. The volume and speed of enunciated letters and words are rising, surging, merging into each other into a crescendo of voices and tones. A conductor might have brought harmony to the symphonies but the two women can only look about in disbelief.

Behind the poetry section, a dishevelled-looking man lies prostrate with the deepest and darkest circles under his eyes. At first he looks crestfallen to see someone else in the room but then he notices the name badges. Colleen kneels to take a closer look. He is much younger than her, perhaps only thirty, but his voice and eyes belong to a much older man.

'I'm looking for a book,' he murmurs.

His voice has a musical quality with a seesaw of notes: it goes up in the middle, then down at the end.

Doris takes in the coal smudged under his smeary blue eyes and knows she must help in whatever way she can. 'Do you know the author?' she asks, in an attempt to be assertive in front of her line manager whom she respects enormously and would like to impress.

'Author?'

His expression suggests he has no idea or is nonplussed. He remains flat on the floor, his feet pointing to opposite sides of the room, a perfect V-shape. As Colleen is calm and collected, Doris assumes this is a regular occurrence.

'Or perhaps the genre, topic? Fiction or non-fiction?'

'Sleep,' he says, full of sibilance, like the S sound is the sweetest sound on any lips.

Doris spots a pale-blue cotton handkerchief protruding from his pocket and a small cut on his hand that looks like it needs Savlon and a plaster. A familiar maternal feeling sweeps over her. Talking seems to exhaust him further so she steps back to give him more air. His hand reaches for the bookshelf to get himself upright but he is clumsy, misses, reaches too late. He topples, turning into a heap of duffle-coat and loafers, emitting a puff sound as he lands in the same place.

'I can search on the computer downstairs, if you like,' Doris offers helpfully, flapping slightly, turning to Colleen for guidance on what on earth to do next.

'To sleep. I just want to sleep.' He still speaks with a musical tone despite the edge of frustration; his sing-song self sounds at odds with the desperation of his sleep-deprived self – only an insomniac is left in the duffle-coat and loafers.

Colleen asks Doris to open his duffle-coat because he looks hot while she retrieves a book from the shelf. Beneath his stubble and his smudgy eyes, he is a truly handsome man. Her calm, purposeful manner soothes Doris. Perhaps this is an ordinary incident here?

The yellow-bound book is called *The Wishing Tale,* a slim volume with a gold-leaf title. Colleen kneels beside the heap as if to pray but immediately starts reading from the book. The crucifix around her neck swings forward. She gestures at Doris to keep stroking the man's brow while she continues to read.

Words begin to fly from the volume in Colleen's hand, as if they circle his head in worship to make a halo around his crown. The word 'slumber' places itself ever so gently on each of his eyelids, and the word 'lullaby' whistles into each ear.

Colleen keeps reading. A tremendous surge of letters, words and sounds make a run for his coat and under his collar. His body makes little wave movements and his head turns to one side. Then a hissing sound envelops the three of them, a low fluting hiss, the gentle but certain beats of a Z. The word 'sleep' dissects itself as if in pre-rapid eye-movement segments to walk up and down his body. A deep satisfying snore emanates from his nose. It is a giant's snore. Doris puts her hand to her mouth, in part to stifle a smile. He is fast asleep. Colleen quietly closes the book.

Into each ear, the events of the day, the week, surge into his brain.

The sound of a camera clicking fills the space as he processes the memories one by one. A spindle peeks out from his ear and discards an unwanted memory like a small pile of the rejected and the painful.

Colleen puts her finger to her lips and ushers Doris to the exit. They don't speak until they are back on the first floor. The sight of the check-in desk and the library stamp brings Doris back to normality with a bump. Colleen takes Doris's hands in hers and looks into her eyes before speaking with such earnestness that Doris feels touched and honoured to be working there with this wonderful woman.

'Sometimes our visitors just need a bedtime story.'

***

Once the customers and the staff vacate the library, Colleen locks the doors for the weekend. Sunday is the worst day of the week for her because the library is closed all day. Nine o'clock on a Monday can't come around fast enough. She tends to pass the time by watching box sets of *Lewis* and *Miss Marple*, drinking sloe gin, rearranging the furniture in the upstairs bedrooms, volunteering as a dog-walker or eBay-ing her husband's smart suits, ties, cuff-links and shoes (time-consuming but cathartic).

Many times she has contemplated going to church – she could fill her day with services at different churches in the morning and evensong. But she feels it's too hypocritical to enter a place of worship when she is an outright SIN-NER. Part of her longs to see familiar faces at the chapel, to sit on a hard pew in her favourite spot near the stained-glass window. But the graveyard is as far as she goes, once a month, just to check the gravestone is still there, that the moss hasn't wormed its way into the inscription she'd thought carefully about: *Godfrey Collect, 1962–2018, remembered forever.*

The truth is, most Sundays she does the exact thing she shouldn't do: nurtures her secret; nestles it in her arms like a stillborn baby; swaddles it in the folds of her bosom though it will never get warm, never make a sound. This Sunday will be different, though, because her friend Andy is coming to her house for the first time. Now that's she's semi-retired, she wants to make more effort with her friends.

The grandfather clock in the hall chimes. She sets off to the graveyard early to give herself plenty of time because she doesn't like to be rushed or late. She wants to bake a cake when she returns because, like her, Andy loves his food.

Since living alone, she's taken to leaving post-it notes in case something happens to her when she is out of the house and no one knows where to find her. She has a drawer full; over time she's found it's possible to recycle them as she rarely goes to new places now that Godfrey isn't around. Perhaps, with time, she might reconnect with her old friends and acquaintances. For now, she has her routines like most people: Sainsbury's; Darwin Library; Suzie's hairdressers. It is sad, really, to think her life can fit so sparingly onto post-it notes in a kitchen drawer.

She keeps the notes brief. *St Chad's graveyard* this one says, flat on the kitchen table, a corner wedged under the pepper pot.

Not rain, but the threat of rain. The colour of the sky whispers it. She'll have to hurry now that she's set off without a brolly. How silly of her. The dampness in the air isn't kind to her hair: a whiff of rain and it mutates into frizz and corkscrews of curls that won't do at all.

Colleen acknowledges the gentleman in an overcoat and cap leaving the churchyard as she enters it. He looks vaguely familiar, perhaps a regular churchgoer as she was before. Before. A tear from his eye connects with a liver-spotted hand. She feels compassion for him, here so early like her, perhaps visiting his dead wife and wondering how he will pass his day. Like her, only she has never experienced grief for her husband. Not really, because in the end, she wasn't much of a wife, more a carer or a prefect burdened with responsibility.

Godfrey's grave is as neat as ever. She imagines him beneath the grass and stones in an apple-pie bed, unable to wriggle. Such a neat place, one body after another, laid in rows. The order of the place rattles Colleen. There is nothing neat or orderly about life, as far as she is concerned, so there shouldn't be in death. Far better to have a random approach to burial to reflect the unpredictability of life and death.

The fake tulips she'd left last time look like they'll manage another month. She tweaks each downcast scarlet face so they look up perkily at the sky and then removes her weeding pad from her handbag. The vertical gravestone always reminds her of him sitting up in bed, his three pillows propping up his torso while his skinny, useless legs were buried under the cover like they'd lost their stuffing.

'Godfrey Collect, 1962–2018, remembered forever. You are still remembered. I'm taking semi-retirement from the library. My replacement has started – Doris – a bit dotty but very good.'

A robin lands on Godfrey's neighbour's gravestone. A portly cherry-red tummy brings a smile to Colleen's face.

'I always come for the same reason, Godfrey. You know why.'

The sound of her voice startles the robin away. Tears of pity, guilt and self-loathing fill Colleen's eyes then dribble down her cheeks. A purple fingernail like a windscreen wiper clears each cheek of water. She says a silent prayer then unfolds her body from the weeding pad to stand. Upright, her six-foot frame towers over the gravestone the way she used to tower over Godfrey's pillow-propped torso to force feed him soup. Tomato on a Monday. Minestrone on the weekend.

'Goodbye, Godfrey. Sleep well.'

Colleen makes it home before the April shower comes down in earnest, which is a relief because she doesn't have to fuss over her hair before Andy arrives. Her little note on the kitchen table welcomes her back. A few hours later she's made a Victoria sponge, which fills the house with warmth and sweetness.

***

Knowing how efficiently she runs the library, Andy has expected her home to be neat, spotlessly clean and tastefully furnished. It is all those things and more. 'What will you do with your spare time? It's quite a change from all the hours you used to work,' he asks.

'I might take up a course – learn a language, or an instrument – and travel a bit, just in the UK. I haven't been to Dorset or Yorkshire in years.' Colleen loads the tray with tea and cake. 'And see more of my friends. That's the most important thing,' she says, smiling at him.

She declines Andy's chivalrous offer to carry the tray of tea and cake and asks him to follow her into the lounge. He likes being in Colleen's kitchen where there is a delicious smell of homemade cake and fresh bread. The cheeses in the greaseproof paper under a glass cloche whet his appetite; there are two jars of homemade pickles and a ramekin dish of butter. It is her house, an elegant townhouse a stone's throw from the town centre, so he dutifully follows her into the lounge. En route, he admires the black-and-white chessboard tiles in the hallway. There's a soothing kind of peace in the house, he muses.

'I'm going to have a party. Semi-retirement is a good reason for one. Just a few friends, nibbles,' she says, as she places the tray on a coffee table and makes herself comfortable in a wing-back chair. The cushion squeezes out each side of her, making a nest against which she can ease her back. 'Get back in touch with people.'

The hospital bed and hoist take up nearly half the space in the lounge and block out most of the light from the lovely bay window. Andy doesn't know where to sit. The hoist looks like the alien out of *War of the Worlds*. Seeing so much metal scaffolding around a bed makes him feel chilly and a little scared that he might catch an illness. By the fact the mattress is stripped bare and there isn't a pillow or cover in sight, he assumes whoever was in that bed won't be climbing back in for a kip anytime soon. Had someone just died here? His cake sticks in his throat until a large gulp of tea swills it into his gullet.

'Great idea. Where will you have it?' He forces the words out while trying to appear comfortable in an upright chair as far away from the bed as possible.

Colleen tucks into a slice of cake, still warm as she touches it carefully with her fingers, oblivious to Andy's bewildered expression. He wishes he was still wearing his hi-vis jacket because a chill has worked its way up his back. The more he tries not to look at the bed, the more his gaze returns to the monstrosity.

Colleen sips her tea, delicately nibbles and chews, like the bed isn't the elephant in the room but more of a unique piece of modern art. 'Oh, here. It's more personal,' she says and waves her arm in a carefree, generous gesture. 'I've always preferred house parties. You?'

Luckily Louis, Andy's chocolate Labrador, saunters in to break the spell. He too looks at the bed and sniffs the metal legs, the mattress, then takes his nose to another part of the lounge before settling beside Andy's leg.

'Not been to many, to be honest. Had a few for Jade when she was little, if that counts. You know, jelly and ice cream and pass the parcel.' He chuckles. 'Got good at making cakes.'

'I've got out of the circle and haven't used my heated buffet server in years! I want to do a bit of socialising now. We used to go to cocktail parties, the occasional dinner party.'

'Was that you and your husband?' Andy asks gently as he strokes Louis's back to comfort himself and his beloved companion.

'He's such a lovely dog,' Colleen responds while playing with the crucifix around her neck, a comment that instigates an update on

Louis's routines and walks from Andy, while he strokes the dog's back repetitively.

'I love dogs,' she says. 'They're so appreciative of kindness and loyal to the end, God bless them. I'll get him a pillow.'

Andy follows Colleen to the music room to look for a pillow, glad of the respite from the lounge and the bed. He can tell the door is normally closed by the captive damp air inside. She reaches for the light switch to alleviate the gloom. Aside from the piano against the back wall, the space is crammed with the paraphernalia that comes with caring for the sick and bedridden – so much metal and plastic bent into curious shapes.

Godfrey's car accident paralysed him; it stole all the best bits that moved and made light. She tended to his bedsores and his hygiene but it wasn't just his spinal cord that was crushed, it was his spirit. He stopped playing the piano. It was the one thing he had done his whole life and for hours after the accident. Playing was the one thing he could still do, unaided, unsupported. They'd had the hoist installed so he could get out of bed into his wheelchair. The piano stool was removed. He sat and played in his wheelchair. He used to complain about not being able to push the pedals with his feet, but the notes kept him alive. Then it stopped. One day he said he hated the sound of the piano. He said it was the voice he could never have again. It mocked him, he said.

When your husband tells you he wants to die, what do you do? Colleen tried all the things she knew: his favourite meals, films, books. It was hopeless. He wouldn't talk about memories or look at the photo albums. He wouldn't have visitors or outside help. He refused to go to church with her. Colleen began to lose her hair; it was the stress. Handfuls of it on her pillow. Then she did a terrible thing. She prayed to God; she prayed Godfrey would die. And he did.

But she doesn't tell Andy these things. She doesn't tell a soul. She reaches inside the room for a pillow and closes the door. 'Do you like chilli?' she asks.

She dashes off into the kitchen. Several freezer bags are defrosting on the kitchen counter. She is still adapting to making suppers for one and occasionally gets the quantities all wrong. Her freezer drawer is full of Godfrey's favourite meals, all by mistake.

Chapter Six

Doris is already thinking about the Sunday-night phone call with Mother as she replenishes the shelves with books from her trolley. For once, she has some good news to tell her about how much she is enjoying her job, even the routine tasks like returning the wanderers to their alphabetised dormitory.

The tricky thing for Doris is getting the units just right before and during the conversation: too much wine and some secret might slop out like an unwelcome blob of porridge; not enough and dry-mouth syndrome stilts the conversation to a funereal hush.

The one thing Doris can say about Mother is that she is consistent: consistent in the time she calls each week and in the unpleasant way in recent years in which she speaks to her only child. Mother didn't want a daughter because daughters were 'beautiful fools'; she'd told Doris as much when she turned forty. The phrase stuck in Doris's brain because Daisy said the same thing about her daughter in *The Great Gatsby,* but she doubted her mother knew she'd quoted F.Scott Fitzgerald. Mother likes reading *Dummies Guides* on all sorts of subjects from keeping hens to quilting, though she doesn't have hens or make quilts.

The trolley lets out its mouse squeak as she parks it by the romance section and hurriedly returns a book to its rightful place. Jane Austen is in the classics section, which Doris feels a bit torn about.

When she told Mother about John and Lisa, her mother was distraught. 'It's all over, isn't it?'

'What's over, Mother?' Doris asked while topping up her units (rosé). She could sense her mother working up to a rant.

'Our bloodline. You've doomed it. When I die, and then you, it will be gone. Forever. Too trusting by half, you are, Doris. You always have been. So much of your time and energy is spent worrying about other people, you forget about yourself.'

I see, thought Doris. So by nature of firstly being born with a vagina, and then marrying a Cock for a husband who left me for a Twat, I have doomed Mother. I am utterly useless.

'Sorry for our suicide, Mother. Did you receive the shortbread I sent you?'

'Oh yes, but it was far too buttery, dear. I have to watch my cholesterol. Why are you talking about suicide? You're not depressed, are you?'

When the phone rings at 6.30 pm, Doris checks that she has everything ready for this week's call. Units: check. Pen and paper: check. Watch: check. She picks up on the fifth ring. Following the all-important update on the state of her mother's corns, the new 'lady doctor' at the local surgery and Iceland's offer on chocolate digestives, Irene is well into the fourth minute.

Doris sits at the kitchen table, gulps down the rest of her units (red) before wedging in her piece of news. 'John's selling the house from under me.'

Doris zones out for a while, unable to deal with what her mother might be saying. Looking at her watch, she sees they've been on the blower for five minutes. Only another one to go and Mother will say it's going to cost her. It is only twenty minutes once a month. Four hours each year. Not a lot to give in the grand scheme of a lifetime but it takes its toll on Doris, on the invisible part of her, her self-esteem.

And then Irene is gone. The long-dead tone of a disconnected line resonates in Doris's ear. It is just a different key to the connection that had gone on minutes before. Doris clears away the debris from the table and tops up her glass with white wine. A little splash of red left in the bottom of the glass makes it swirl into a gentle rose colour. She toasts herself and knocks it back in one.

Since Cock left, Doris has developed fads, cravings, munchies, generally late at night or very early in the morning and often, strangely, involving foods beginning with M. Marmite. Maltesers. Malbec. Mince pies. So marvellous to have her hankerings satisfied without a damp paw or limb in sight. Doris often smiles at the ceiling at that thought.

Now that middle age means she has to get up for a piss two or three times a night, she gets to listen to her late-at-night speaking clock friend at all hours. And see the moon. She's spent years watching the insides of her eyelids instead of something so completely beautiful and amazing on the other side of her curtains. Her routine on sleepless

35

nights (which is often) is to pull the bedroom curtain ajar so she and the moon can look at one another, free from self-consciousness, because the moon does not criticise her every move. Not like Mother.

***

By the time Andy gets to Margaret's house, he is starting to flag a bit. The roads to the suburb of Monksmoor were congested, and the sausage-and-egg sandwich he'd wolfed down for lunch didn't suit him. Since he'd been close to one of his favourite truck stops, it didn't do not to eat something. Old habits die hard.

Andy and Margaret have been on first-name terms for some time. Like him, she takes her time to get to know people. Margaret always says he's a sight for sore eyes as he comes bustling into the kitchen in his hi-vis jacket with his yellow trays and workman's gloves, full of purpose. It's their routine, a little scene from married life that they play out. He's happy to go along with it and knows the script. He likes Margaret, and he likes making people happy. She'd pushed the boat out the night before by booking a double delivery slot. And an extra pack of four mince-pies from the bakers at Stan's Supermarket, Andy's employer. On special offer but still an indulgence for Margaret.

'No swaps this week, Margaret.'

Her hands rummage through the tray like she is playing lucky dip, rummage, rummage, rummage.

'I see you've booked back to back.' Andy collapses his lanky legs into a kitchen chair like a giraffe. 'Is everything alright?'

'Got it! I'll make us a cup of tea to go with our mince pies. I've ordered an extra pack. How many sugars do you want this time?'

'As it's a special occasion and a Friday, I'll have three.'

There is the long thin sound of the zip on Andy's hi-vis jacket and then the click of the kettle as it reaches the spot. The teaspoon tinkle-tinkles inside each mug, which makes Margaret think of the twitters her pupils used to make when she read them a funny Dahl story. She and Andy do companionable silence well, she thinks, as she pushes her hair behind one ear. She is wearing pearl earrings.

Andy removes his watch and plonks it by his mug of tea on the kitchen table. Double slot or not, he has less than ten minutes to get to the bottom of Margaret's extravagance of extra mince pies and a double slot.

Having taken early retirement from teaching, she moans all the time about the cost of things. The shapes, colours, and packaging from her weekly shop are strewn across the kitchen units like children's faces. The routine of ordering the same packages makes her feel in control of her life after suddenly having so much time on her hands and no one to tell her how to spend it. He notices a new fridge magnet which says *Seize the Day*.

'I think I should get out a bit more. Socially.' Margaret waits for a response. It seems a long time coming. 'What do you think?'

Andy sticks out his bottom lip. 'Why not?' He reaches for another mince pie. 'Especially now the weather's warming up.'

'There's a film I'd like to see starring Emma Thompson. I wonder if you'd like to see it with me?'

With his mouth full he says, 'I only watch romcoms, but thanks for the offer. Mince pies are good. It's nice to eat them out of season. I like Julia Roberts.'

Margaret shuffles her feet: she's put on her best shoes and they are pinching her little toe. Andy shoves the last piece of pie into his mouth and washes it down with the dregs of tea. She sees that he is about to get up to go. Margaret reaches for the kettle to refill it with water. There is a bunch of daffodils on the window ledge and the sugar bowl, recently refilled, matches the mugs.

'There's another pack of mince pies. Would you like one warmed?'

'I need to go. Jade's coming round for supper. Thanks for the brew and mince pie.'

As she watches him rise from the chair, she spots a crumb-like beauty spot hanging to the left side of his mouth where his beard is thick and coarse. She thinks there is a dimple beneath it, a small dent when his mouth expands into a grin. She doesn't know whether to say anything or not. She decides to wipe her lip instead.

'See you the same time next week.' At least he's reliable she thinks.

As soon as the front door closes behind him, she removes her shoes and earrings and heats up two mince pies in the microwave to eat one after the other.

***

Outside Andy's semi-detached house, a couple walk by hand in hand making small talk, their breath forming one large empty speech bubble. A little girl with rosy cheeks strokes a cat while her mother finds the correct change for the bus, number 64, which will probably take them into Shrewsbury town centre for a meal out. High heels in a hurry overtake them after a long day at work. The streetlights are just hints of amber light on a grey canvas, competing with headlights as the sky threatens darkness. People rush from one place to the next in pursuit of warmth and light, oblivious to what's inside the curtains at number 15 Heap Street, close to a park where Andy and Jade spent many hours.

Even in his recliner in the take-off position, Andy rarely keeps still when his daughter Jade comes over on a Friday night to watch *The Jeremy Kyle Show,* her favourite chat show.

She presses the mute button when the adverts appear. Andy presses the button for an upright position for a pit-stop. 'I'll make us a brew.'

Jade rearranges the lacey pillow behind her back and the soft fleece which has slipped off her bare feet. Manicured blue fingernails edged with glitter scroll through the messages on her phone. Suddenly she inhales sharply. Gratified, she looks around the living room she'd thrown her heart and soul into decorating nine years earlier when she lived with her dad; it's still completely unchanged. She contemplates whether the enormous heart-shaped mirror above the hearth and the fairy lights strewn from one end to the other would look nice in her bedsit.

'Kit-Kat Chunky?' Andy shouts from the kitchen with his mouth full.

'No, thanks.' And nor should he, especially after a fish-and-chip supper, but she doesn't say so. 'Amy's had a miscarriage.'

'Never met her.'

'Nor have I. She's uploaded a photo of a tiny coffin.'

'God, streuth. She should write something like that in a diary.'

'She'll feel empowered now she's shared it.'

'With potentially millions of weirdos who don't give a damn?'

'I'm not a weirdo. I care.'

Jade removes the tie-backs from the lounge curtains, regretting her decision not to send poor Amy an emoji face. The tie-backs were made specially because the curtains, as thick as whipped cream, concealed too much of the double-glazed window. She can see how they are a bit over the top for a semi on the less fashionable side of Shrewsbury but at the time she was in love – or she thought she was – with Tommy, a new boy at school with a skateboard and a tattoo of a clown.

The fake fire doesn't provide enough light in the room now, so she tries the switch for the main light: a chandelier with dangling crystals and candles, a statement piece worth the inconvenience to Dad and visitors over five foot ten.

'The bulbs have gone!' she says, and turns on the lava lamp she'd once coveted and a side-lamp with a pink tasselled shade. Looking up, she can see there isn't a single bulb in the chandelier.

Andy plonks the cup of tea onto a glass-topped side-table. 'It's got sugars in.'

Jade immediately picks it up to place a coaster underneath. 'Do you like the decor here, Dad?'

Andy sticks out his bottom lip as he looks around the room like he hasn't seen it before. 'Can't say I notice. It was all your doing.' He takes a slurp of tea like it's amber nectar. 'You'd be about fifteen, I think.' A private memory makes him smile.

'That's what I mean.' Jade presses the mute button again and the three faces on the screen are immediately de-gagged. They're all talking at once: 'He's such a loser! Fancy telling millions of viewers you're having an affair before telling your wife!' Cleansed of guilt and free from moral criticism, the show moves onto another participant willing to over-share regrets in exchange for free therapy.

Andy travels back in his reclining chair and looks at the strong tea in the mug in his hand. The mug is a gift from Colleen; it's one of the few items in the house that isn't pink. It was a thank-you present but he can't quite remember why. Fixing a few shelves in the library, that was most likely it.

'Do you know what my biggest regret is, Dad?'

'Do you know mine?'

The programme will end soon and then Jade will probably be off home. He'll listen to a few tracks of soul music before bed. He glances at his watch. He sees Jade has drawn the curtains, which she doesn't usually do. He prefers them open, even at night, so that he can see the photographs on the window ledge of himself and Jade. The one of her in a swing in Jubilee Park is his favourite. He pushed her higher and higher and she giggled and he laughed. He sometimes thinks about that moment when he drives by Jubilee Park on a Monday to deliver a weekly shop to Mr Howarth. The other photos are just of Jade because he was behind the camera; his wife Catherine had left them by then.

'No!' Jade tuts between sips of tea. 'A lie-detector test!'

Over the years Andy has perfected the art of zoning out noise. It started when Jade used to fake cry, later when she listened to pop music, talked all hours on the phone; then she moved out and it was hellishly quiet, except on Fridays when she visits him.

Andy eventually realises Jade's switched off the TV and the fake flames.

'What do you want for your birthday, Dad?'

There's no protruding lip; there's no thought. Andy shakes his head. 'Save your money. I expect you'll be getting a deposit together for a house.'

'Not yet. I've just booked a fortnight in Tenerife.' She checks her nails are still perfectly blue.

'I'll walk you home,' he says, reaching for his hi-vis jacket he wears for work while wondering who's she going on holiday with. But he doesn't ask because she'd say he was prying into her business. If he was on Facebook, he might know.

A whiff of salt and vinegar carries from the kitchen down the hall. Andy regrets having an extra sausage on the side of fish and chips.

Jade tosses a compact mirror into her studded handbag and arranges the faux-leather strap on her left shoulder. 'Dad, there's no need. I've got a lift.'

She'd meant to tell him about Bosh at the start of the evening but the right moment didn't seem to come along. All her mates know because they're on Facebook – and her hairdresser, of course, because she knows everything about her. Now the doorbell is ringing and she's run out of time.

Jade stands on tiptoes in her cowboy boots to kiss her dad's cheek just beneath his eye where it's beard-free. He stands and waits for the door to open so he can get a look at her latest boyfriend. They don't tend to last long for one reason or another, but he always likes to meet them.

A whiff of cold air and Jade closes the door behind her before he gets a chance to see the man, let alone speak to him. Footsteps, a titter, the car doors opening and closing. He shrugs his shoulders and heads back to the lounge to listen to Ray Charles pour his heart out.

Chapter Seven

Jubilee Park. Friday's Garage. Home Supplies. Nania's Nails. Spring Avenue.

Mr Winston Howarth's residential mobile home is at the far end of Spring Avenue, the only one with a soft-top car parked outside. Two years ago, he'd had the car customised so he could drive it with one leg – not that you'd know that by looking at the car – but it hasn't moved in more than twelve months because walking from the house to the car is difficult. The MG has its own cover like a rain hat that ties in a bow under the chin.

A year before the car was customised, Winston's operation on his leg went wrong. An infection spread, tragically resulting in an amputation that rendered a terrible loss to a man who took pride in his independence as a widower. There were so many challenges, like pushing a shopping trolley. Then Winston got clued up on internet shopping and got Andy to deliver his groceries from Stan's Supermarket.

Andy slams his van into reverse to line up the rear end with Mr Howarth's back gate. He once showed Mr Howarth the customised cup holders and seats in his van. Stan's Supermarket has a small team of self-employed drivers with vans for local deliveries. It suits Andy better than long-distance hauls now he's fifty-two, but he keeps some of the habits he had as a trucker: fry-ups in choice truck stops, and a single bed only a few inches wider and longer than his cab bed used to be. Anything else feels too big.

Like a lot of Andy's customers, Mr Howarth orders much the same every week. He's a cake man, though you wouldn't think it to look at his tiny frame; he is seventy, very frail, though he's not one to complain about feeling old, ill or finding his prosthetic leg heavy and cumbersome. Once Andy had lifted it and was surprised by its sturdy weight.

Despite the difficulties of living alone, Mr Howarth is always smartly dressed in a modern, freshly-ironed shirt, and he perches on a bar stool in his tiny kitchen like he's Val Doonican entertaining a live audience. Last time Andy came, Mr Howarth showed him his new iPhone. He said he liked to keep up to date, which is why he always has Radio One on – just on low, mind.

Although it's only six o'clock, the light has faded. Neighbours have their lights on and some curtains are drawn. There's a smell of cooking. There's one more delivery and then home for dinner. Car headlights approach Andy then the engine stops and the lights close their eyes. It'll be summer soon, he thinks, as he checks Mr Howarth's order is complete, and then he'll be delivering food for BBQs and garden parties.

The news is on next door. The light comes and goes from the TV. Andy focuses on carrying the tray to the back door, where he places it on the stone wall. There's a blob of red on one of the stone steps and another on the flagstone path.

'Mr Howarth, it's Andy, from Stan's. Are you there? I've got your groceries.'

Another set of headlights approach and park up. People are back from work, settling in for the evening. The concern is already working its way into Andy's heart. He knocks and knocks and then opens the door. Teddy, Mr Howarth's elderly boxer, barges passed him to relieve himself on the stones. A waft of dog shit from inside says it's a little too late.

The trail of blood spots continues into the kitchen, dark-red splashes on the light linoleum floor, a broken plate and cup, a checked T-towel covered in blood. Andy tiptoes between the blood, shit and the debris into the lounge. He's not been further than the kitchen before and he calls out with each step because he feels like a trespasser.

Mr Howarth's prosthetic leg leans against the sofa, resting itself like its having a breather before going to bed. Teddy returns and pants outside what must be Mr Howarth's bedroom door. Andy knocks once and opens the door, sweating profusely because of the overpowering heat from the radiators and the fear of what might be inside.

Teddy barges in first, using his boxer strength to nudge Andy out of the way. Mr Howarth has collapsed in his wheelchair beside his soiled bed. Without his leg, teeth or clothes. Andy has to take a moment before he can speak or act. He fumbles for his phone to call for an ambulance while using his free hand to pull a soiled sheet off the bed to cover the flaccid willy stuck into a plastic container once used for margarine. He checks for a pulse.

'Yes, he's still breathing. Winston Howarth. Spring Avenue. It's laboured, though. Number 15 – hurry up. There's sick and shit everywhere and he's banged his head. It's not bleeding now, no – but it has been. A lot.'

Mr Howarth has tended to a bang to the head with loo roll and sticky tape; it's a pitiful sight. Andy gently touches his arm, which is a ladybird of age spots. It's warm to the touch. Teddy moans then places his head on Winston's lap and wags his docked tail.

Winston's eyes suddenly open. 'Can you feed him?' The eyes are watery and the gaze is sad, distant.

Andy replenishes Teddy's bowls and opens a fresh packet of Victoria sponge. He warms the milk in the microwave to help Winston keep it down. He's glad to be doing something helpful and rushes, quickly, fearful Winston might slip away while he's out of the room.

'When did you last have something to eat or drink, Mr Howarth?' he asks, while helping him to sip from the glass.

'Call me, Winston.' Mr Howarth rubs the side of his head, perhaps remembering it hurts. 'Yesterday, I think. Or the day before. I had a fall outside, picking up Teddy's poo.'

'Is there anyone I can call for you?'

Winston shakes his head mournfully and carefully inserts a bite of cake to suck on. Does he usually get dressed especially for Andy? The thought is too painful to hang onto. The man is childlike and ancient at the same time.

'He's a good boy,' he says and pats Teddy on the back. The dog's wand of a tail is frantic at the slightest touch of his master's hand. 'Bless him,' he says weakly, like every word is an effort.

Winston smiles. Andy thinks it's the smile of a child, open and full of wonder. He's an old, sick man and yet the purity of his smile and the happiness behind it bring a knot to Andy's throat. He brings more warm milk and cake and a pillow to put behind Winston's back. He opens the bedroom window and avoids looking too closely around the room. Perhaps the old man will recover, he hopes.

The ambulance arrives to confirm that Winston's vital signs are fine; he won't be admitted. *Just keep an eye on him.* Andy is still wearing his hi-vis jacket with Stan's Supermarket on the back, so it seems pointless trying to say anything else except thanks. Over-running, Andy calls HQ to explain what has happened.

Andy closes the window at Winston's request. 'I've got one delivery and then I'll be straight back to call on you, Winston. Are you comfortable?'

'Take Teddy with you. He needs a change.'

Teddy makes himself comfortable on the front passenger seat and they set off. Less than two hours later they are back, parked in exactly the same spot. The silver moon and inquisitive stars are above; it will be a cold night.

Leaving Teddy in the van, Andy makes his way in through the kitchen, through the lounge, into the bedroom. Mr Howarth's bedside light is still on but he isn't in his wheelchair. His body is spread-eagled in bed, naked, bathed in lemon light.

Half a glass of milk and the remains of a slice of Victoria sponge are on the bedside table for the man without a pulse. The bed is a den of shit, piss, vomit; the indignity and loneliness of Winston's death bring Andy to tears. He forgets he is almost a stranger, a delivery man; he is all Mr Howarth has got – had got.

He opens cupboards in the spare bedroom to find a clean sheet to cover the emaciated body. The quietness of the house is too horrible. To Andy, there is only Winston's dog Teddy, awake and waiting at this tragic hour. The door to Winston's wardrobe is ajar, where his pressed shirts hang waiting for a visitor. Andy opens the window again because the stench and heat are overpowering. He has never seen a dead body before, and he doesn't know what to do with his feelings of anger and grief.

Andy perches beside his customer, the elderly gentleman who loved his cake, and he weeps. Before calling the ambulance again, he feels brave enough to close Mr Howarth's eyes.

'There's no rush this time. He's dead.'

It is close to midnight before he and Teddy leave the scene of the crime. There's a key to 15 Spring Avenue under the back-door mat because Andy didn't know what to do with it. No one seems to care Mr Howarth has died except Andy and Teddy.

***

Still smelling of shower gel, Jade lets herself into her dad's house as she still has a key on her pink pom-pom key ring. Surprised not to see him having breakfast at his usual hour, she calls up the stairs. When there's no answer, she peers into each room until she finds him still in bed. The house has three bedrooms: one double and two singles. They've never talked about it but Andy sleeps in a single room, little more than a box room.

'Everything alright, Dad? It's nearly nine o'clock.'

'Yes, thanks.' He sits up as she opens the curtains. 'Quite a late night – got watching a film, as you do.' He pulls up the duvet over his bare chest. The room is cramped, especially with the door open and two big dogs.

'Why've you got another dog in here?' Jade says in a bad-tempered voice.

'A neighbour's – just dog-sitting for a bit.'

'He stinks. Just wondered if I should ask Bosh to join us on Friday night?'

Andy feels tired. The sight of Winston's dead body has haunted him for most of the night. Teddy cried for hours, between farting and snoring and sniffing Louis. A kind of anger has taken Andy by surprise; it's still with him in the morning.

'Are you listening to me, Dad?' Jade's hand is on her hip; now it's moving the strap on her handbag further up her shoulder. 'Are you sure you're alright?'

Andy sees the little girl she was, impatient, on the verge of throwing a paddy over a chocolate bar he'd eaten, stamping her foot. She hasn't changed. Teddy lets out a long howl from the bottom of the bed where he's taken refuge. Louis tries his best to ignore him.

'I'll see you and Bob on Friday then,' he says, as brightly as he can muster for his lovely daughter.

'It's Bosh, Dad. Bosh. Just this once, shave. Please.' She closes the door to his box room.

Teddy howls again, louder than before. Andy takes it as a cue to get up and do something, so he gets dressed. With the dawning

46

realisation that Teddy will be staying with him indefinitely until he has a better idea, he retrieves the key from under Winston's mat. Before he lets himself into the mobile home, he glances at Teddy who is watching him from the front seat in the van. His face is more wrinkled and worried-looking than normal for a boxer, which is saying something.

Andy wants to be in and out as soon as possible. He feels like a thief. He collects Teddy's bed, bowl and toys. The place has a strange quiet, as if it has spoken and is still waiting for a reply. Like it remembers what's happened and can't talk about it. It's like a naughty Jade who used to steal sweets after dinner, buttoning up her mouth but looking shamefaced anyway.

The food Andy had optimistically unpacked and stored just the day before is still in the kitchen cupboards. The packaging looks like hostages. In one cupboard he finds some tins of dog food and a bag of dry food to take home for Teddy.

Something makes him take a peek inside the lounge before he leaves. The prosthetic leg still leans against the sofa, waiting to be taken out for a jaunt, and a pair of pants and brown socks hang limply from the radiator.

He leaves the key under the mat for a serendipitous burglar, throws Teddy's items in the van and drives away with Winston's best friend beside him.

Chapter Eight

Andy bangs on the window to get Colleen's attention. She is standing under the check-out sign in the Darwin library looking frayed. She's a colour-coordinated lady: her fingernails match the colour of her jumper dress, a purple and cosy navy number with a dark purple scarf. The ten purple fingernails jump to her face to conceal her open mouth at the sight of Andy and a strange dog walking through the library's double doors.

'Andy! You can't come in with a dog unless you're partially sighted. What's happened to Louis?'

Andy briefly explains how he's come to have an elderly boxer dog with an endearing howl and a sad expression. Some of the regulars in the far reaches of the library (where many spend their day, especially in inclement weather) come over to fuss Teddy. Andy smiles; Teddy looks happier to have the company and fuss.

Colleen strokes his narrow fawn back and suddenly her face brightens. 'I know! Bring him in.'

In need of a new audiobook, Andy is only too pleased to be allowed in. He likes the library; it's a social outing of sorts but without too much talking. Colleen sends him off in one direction while she briskly heads to the children's area with Teddy, taking control of the situation in the way she does so well.

This month the theme is 'under the sea' in the children's library. The bookshelves are in the shape of shells above tiny pearl chairs with trailing seaweed and seagrass. Mats segregate the sea-blue carpet in the shape of a mermaid, a pirate and a dolphin. A volunteer comes in twice a week to read to the children when Colleen can't do it; she's called Sandy, though her hair isn't the colour or texture of sand. Thoughtfully, she's wearing red boots as she is reading *The Pirate Ship* to a group of small bodies on the carpet.

Once the children have stopped cheering and fist-pumping at the happy ending of the story, Colleen takes Teddy into the circle. She explains he is a very special story dog. An expectant hush and wide eyes greet them. Teddy's doe eyes and sad, grumpy expression win them over in minutes.

Fortuitously, Colleen remembered reading about the use of dogs to help reluctant readers. Teddy the Story Dog could be a great new initiative to liven the place up a bit, especially as the number of children who regularly visit the library is dwindling and pressure is afoot to reduce the stock of children's books, which Colleen wants to fight all the way.

Sam, a little boy of about eight, is tugging at his mother's hand to go home but, after Colleen's explanation, his mother Justine is keen to try it (anything is worth a try once!). Colleen selects a book based on the little she learns about Sam and the four of them head to the old school room on the second floor. It takes a while for Sam to get over the excitement of being in the same room as a dog, as they only have a hamster at home. A very small one called Herbert.

Colleen talks to Sam through Teddy, and he begins to settle. 'Teddy doesn't know what the book is about. What does the front cover tell us?'

Dear Teddy, he so loves the company and attention. He is tired after so much coming and going after normally being on his own or asleep or panting and whining outside Winston's bedroom. But he keeps going.

Sam tries to talk about the book in a way no one has expected. Colleen asks Justine to write a few comments about the experience and suggestions for going forward. Little Sam looks so pleased with himself; he hugs Teddy before scampering off much happier than he was before.

'We've been having a lovely time together, haven't we, Teddy?' Colleen passes the lead to Andy, but he doesn't take it immediately.

Teddy's docked tail, like a miniature wand, waves and makes a silent tinkle, tinkle sound as if spreading fairy dust on the library carpet. It seems like he wants to stay.

'He's a great dog. Make someone a lovely companion.' Andy pauses. 'He and Louis get on alright but I can't have the two big dogs at home and in the van with me. '

Colleen smiles as she gives Teddy a gentle pat. Godfrey didn't like dogs but now he's gone, perhaps a good dog like Teddy would be company for her. 'Text me your address and I'll pick him up after work. We'll give it a try.'

***

Later that day, Colleen laughs when she walks into Andy's lounge, narrowly missing her head on the chandelier. 'I like a man in touch with his feminine side. It's very Mills and Boon.'

Andy blushes under his beard. 'Jade was a girlie-girl. Still is. I think her new fella thinks I'm gay! I'm not, by the way.'

'Have you met Doris yet?' Colleen asks, one hand stroking Teddy, the other Louis who is suffering from having his nose pushed out of joint by Teddy's arrival. The new dog's smell is everywhere.

'No. Doris must have been upstairs. I got myself a new audiobook – Frederick Forsyth.'

'Not my cup of tea but you'll like it. Doris is a bit of a find. Very well read – and she entertained our reading group no end on Angela Carter and Penelope Lively! I'll probably spend more time in the children's section now Doris is on board. She prefers the adult market.'

'Tea, wine, or do you want to a lift home with Teddy and his bits and bobs? Or all three?'

***

Doris is convinced that an aerial photograph of the area would show a white space for her house; a ghost's house; a space-bar pause between the terraced houses each side of her anonymous life with a sign suspended from nothing saying 'For Sale'. Tina's house would be there with her yellow Beetle parked outside. And the house of the couple who moved in in the new year who hold hands all the time. Their house would be there. But number 42? She didn't think so.

Doris returns home in the light after an early finish at the library. It is a relief not to feel frightened by the dark on the walk along Utkinton Road to her house, but once she sees the FOR SALE sign above her front door she remembers what's happened to her life and what is going to happen any time soon. Then she wishes – wishes hard – that it was pitch black, so black that she couldn't see it. It is easy to forget about it when she is inside or at work but there it is, right there to greet her. A really warm welcome home from Cock. FOR SALE.

No one seems interested in the place. Tina says he's asking too much for it, getting what he deserved for not decorating and siphoning off the best of the place. The price has been dropped by £5,000, and there has been one viewing while Doris, luckily, was at work. She put her dirty underwear in the washing basket that day to be 'cooperative'.

Doris manages to get into the hall before releasing the avalanche of sobs that kick her to the hall carpet. On her knees, between the tears and the thundering jerks of air her mouth and lungs fight over, she notices something different about the hall carpet.

It is clean.

Someone has been into her house.

Standing up, she marches into the lounge. The tray of food is not there. Her Jenga stacks of books serving as coffee tables are stacked neatly in one corner of the room. In the kitchen, the washing up has been washed, put away. The bin isn't over-spilling or stinking.

Doris runs upstairs. Her bed is made. The bedroom carpet is visible. The bathroom smells of bleach and something lemony is swimming in the toilet.

Did Cock clean? Surely not! If not him, then who? Then it comes to her. The sordid truth. It was Twat. She still has a key. Once her best friend, they'd shared everything. Twat has cleaned. Not to be nice, no, but to get the place straight so she and Cock can get as much for the house as possible.

Doris kicks the wastepaper bin along the landing. It rolls along, having been annoyingly emptied of its waste. What did Twat ripple her fingers through in her absence? The indignity of it turns her face red.

Once she's stopped crying Doris thinks about the broken oven, the tired carpets, the dated kitchen and the hateful bathroom, and she asks herself if she wants to stay in the same house where she lost her husband, best friend and unborn child? The bathroom floor will always be red, red, red.

They make her drink. Guzzle until her stomach is a well, so full it begins to pour over the top and trickle down Utkinton Street, a red rivulet, an S shape all the way to the corner shop and back. They still make her drink, sip it if she has to, faces at the bottom of the glass.

She keeps drinking, swaying, and they are still watching. Then it is dark, the colour of a drinker's liver.

***

Andy is halfway through his business in the bathroom when he turns to the property section in the local paper, *The Shropshire Star*. It is there in black and white: 15 Spring Avenue, Shrewsbury, for sale. £65,000, a two-bedroom mobile home with a spacious drive and modern kitchen. Winston's home. If Winston has next of kin, they will be selling the house.

He wants to speak to a family member more than anything, but he knows the chance of an estate agent divulging that kind of information to him is unlikely, so there and then he decides to pose as a cash-buyer looking for a property for his mother (God rest her soul in heaven).

The viewing is arranged for Monday afternoon, close to the time he used to deliver to dear Mr Howarth when he was alive.

'It's priced for a quick sale,' Sandra says, as she unlocks the back door in her comfortable but smart work shoes. 'It's just been cleaned right through, as you can probably tell.'

He can tell even before he steps inside because the bloodstains on the step have gone. 'I'll just take a look outside first.'

For the first time, Andy walks round to the back where he can dry his eyes without the estate agent watching. He follows the flagstones to the small area of gravel and flagstones where Teddy used to do his business, the spot where Winston fell. There are faint patches of what could be blood, but he can't be sure. He catches a glimpse of Sandra watching him from the window in the spare bedroom where he found the clean sheet. He puts his hands in his pockets and pretends to contemplate the view from the garden. Winston's customised sports car has gone.

Someone has packed up Winston's life, hosed it down from top to bottom, then rebranded and added his home to a marketing list with a modest price tag. The gravel crunches under his boots as he walks back the way he came. He has Jade, Louis, Colleen, a few friends and customers who need him. Winston was adamant he had no one in his hour of need and yet, from the efficient cleaning up and marketing of his home, someone is alive and pulling strings. Who?

52

Inside the lounge, there is a photograph of Winston and what must have been his wife, Maureen. Andy remembers him talking about her. She had a dirty laugh, Winston said. Cancer stole her some time ago when she was quite young. There are several photos of Teddy taken at various ages, confirming his old age now. Beside one picture of Teddy before his muzzle turned grey, a dark-haired girl in a graduation gown smiles at the camera. Her head is tilted at an angle.

The pants and socks from the radiator have been removed and a rug placed to conceal the stains on the lounge carpet. Andy moves slowly into the first bedroom, an innocuous space used for storage. He gives the bathroom a cursory glance then sticks his head into Winston's bedroom. The mattress has been removed, his wheelchair and prosthetic limb taken to someplace new. The room has been sanitised.

Andy forces himself to open the door to the fitted wardrobe. When the redundant hangers sway and jostle, he could cry. He thinks about the tenuous threads of self-respect in the fibres in those shirts, in the upright posture Winston held on his stool, in the small talk he made to his delivery man. He is sure of it now, how Winston had dressed for his visit, thought of it as a social occasion. He wipes away a tear.

'I like it a lot. I'm interested in the furniture too. Perhaps pass my number onto the owner so we can talk directly.'

Andy forgets himself and makes to step into the kitchen where Winston kept a pen and notepad beside his pills. He normally jotted down items of food, stuff for Teddy, that kind of thing. Once he'd left a note for Andy to say thank you for the delivery because he was in bed with a cold and was sorry to miss him. At the time, Andy had noticed Winston hadn't taken his pills for Monday, so he'd taken them through with a glass of water and the old man had swallowed them reluctantly. The last time Andy was here the box was full. Winston hadn't taken a single pill in a week.

'I can't promise but I'll certainly pass the message on, Mr Love. We've got your number on file.'

'I'd like to know what they've got to say before thinking about my offer.'

Chapter Nine

After drinking a fruity bottle of rosé with a decent alcohol percentage, Doris slept soundly, but at two o'clock in the morning she wakes with a jolt, the electric-shock kind that takes a while to get over.

Her dream taps at her consciousness as she orientates herself in the room; she recalls the presence of books in an illegible form, words that were inky deposits like squashed insects. Books were piled high in gigantic towers around her, trapping her in the confines of their pages and her ignorance. Then a God-like voice said, 'Who is it, love?' and the books tumbled, morphing into fallen leaves on their journey to the ground. And then a stork joined her. Feathers dispersed all around her bare feet and chicks morphed into babies with wings. She opened out her arms, which were branches bereft of leaves and birds.

She opens the curtains to expose a half-moon in an anthracite sky, just her and the moon stuck in the night's throat. Hostages. Is John awake? Is he making love to Lisa? The sun will eventually toss Doris a rope to heave her into a new day further away from this tortuous life-and-death moment.

It's a Wednesday night. Not a going-out kind of night, so the pavements and the road are deserted except for sleeping cars and badly parked scooters. The twenty-four-hour Tesco will be open. Perhaps she could browse the shelves to kill a few hours? Buy a box of Maltesers or two to eat in bed. She rubs her arms beneath the cotton skin of her nightie; it looks cold outside. Perhaps not.

Doris climbs back into bed to read *Birthday Letters* until she nods off, the sidelight left on, the curtains ajar. The sun does throw her a rope but she doesn't notice until the alarm startles her awake. They are expecting a delivery of new books at the library, so she rushes to get ready and arrives half an hour early, spurred on by the smell of a new book, the feel of its crisp pages and firm spine, a sense of newness, undiscovered voices. It's one of the few things in her life which still excites her. Dr Timpson said that might be due to her medication, which evens out a lot of the ups and downs. When he said that, she'd looked into his lovely, caring face and thought of a flat line going beeeeeeeeep.

The Man Booker Prize longlist has been announced, so the library will be stocking some of the titles. The new Poet Laureate has also just been named, promoting a display of poetry on the ground floor. Colleen takes charge of the children's library with the help of volunteer, Frederick. They will be promoting the titles of the new Children's Laureate and the Carnegie winner Elizabeth Acevedo.

Delivery of new books also means disposing of books that have lost their appeal to the ground floor. Some are donated, others sold off for 10p. As a member of staff, she has the privilege to roam in the passageways and the labyrinth of stairs to the basement where books are consigned to archive, oblivion, an author's graveyard. It's not a job she likes.

On the first floor, Doris feels a flutter of excitement when she sees a book she has read: *The Betrayal of Trust* by Susan Hill. There are times when she comes across a book she hasn't read and wishes she had – perhaps as an angst-ridden teenager, or a single woman, a pregnant woman. So often an author can make someone feel like they're not alone.

The library doesn't have high shelves requiring ladders anymore, though it did at one time which would have been fun for some. The shelves are mostly dark wood, some sturdier than others, perhaps reconstituted from something bulky. Doris traces her fingers across the spines on the bottom shelf in fiction, a level some customers fail to browse because it's not in their eye-line; certainly some of the older readers avoid bending or kneeling at all costs. It's a shelf that gets dustier than others. She feels sorry for authors with a surname beginning with F or U who are placed at ankle height. One day she might be there, not under G for Gambol but under her maiden name.

The tinnitus of technology is louder than usual today: the photocopier is in use and Colleen is printing off material to promote 'chatter and natter' on a Thursday afternoon, and Scrabble on a Monday morning. Sydney is here on his scooter, which has an unusually loud beep for reversing. IT drop-in is popular today; it's often the same faces but the tutor, Chris – a lovely volunteer with big hands – has two new worried faces to show the basics. The small reading and study area by the computers provides a home for newspapers and magazines. Those that want to study will sometimes sit at a desk wearing an expression that says they are reading for duty. An assignment or research, perhaps. A young lady is there now, reading with a pencil in her mouth.

Colleen hurries into the children's area moments before the guided reading for the under-fives starts. A boy with a Peter-Pan expression rushes up to her excitedly. In the romance section, Doris's eye catches a face close to tears; the reader has come to the end of her book. She squeezes up her eyes to read the title but she can only make out the word *The*. The elegantly dressed woman closes the book and places it on her lap. She is bereft, satisfied and unsatisfied at the same time. Doris knows how it feels to come to the end of a great book. Coming back to reality with a bump and losing a best friend all at the same time; it's a lot to deal with.

Doris hops into the lift to the second floor with a handful of new books to display in the old school room. She holds the pristine books as carefully as a newborn and thinks of both babies and books as sources of light. But she can only ever experience the one kind.

Hours later, at the end of the working day, she steps outside to the azure sky, to the sound of cars, horns, footsteps, but the only visual impressions from the universe outside the library are the red lupins, scarlet roses and crimson poppies nestling in the flower bed and draping from the hanging baskets — red red red. The fire of summer is everywhere. Even suburbia has turned red – the letterbox, the stop sign, the sound of a siren.

The strange sense of metamorphosis continues at home when Tina calls round to show Doris her new hair. She has turned into a mermaid overnight. 'Hair extensions. Aren't they fab!' She twists her head and the hair obediently swishes in a carousel around her face. 'Do you fancy a few highlights?'

Tina has mentioned highlighting Doris's auburn hair several times before to brighten up the nocturnal look she has. 'No, thanks.'

'I bought you a present.' Tina hands her a tube of cream for cracked heels. 'It's sandals weather,' she says by way of explanation.

'Your lisp's gone,' Doris says, astonished.

'I let my tongue heal up. The infection made it smell.'

Doris wrinkles her nose. Tina gets up to go and then has a thought. 'Tomorrow you go into work late, so I wondered if you fancy looking at a few houses together? It's an honest way to snoop in someone else's house, have a laugh, and it might give you a few ideas about where you want to move to. And décor.'

'Are you moving?' Doris asks, rubbing her eyes after a long day.

'No, but you are.'

Bedtimes in the summer haven't been so bad so far. The double bed still feels like a king size but when it's not cold she doesn't miss John's warmth so much. Until he'd gone, she hadn't realised what a wonderful hot-water bottle his big body was.

The following crisp morning Doris sees Tina coming down Telford Street, so she ducks down an alleyway between two houses and holds her breath until she walks by. A large cloud of air expels from her mouth like a dragon. A bus chugs by, which makes Doris feel more at home in her skin – until she turns the corner into Getting Street and a mum is pushing a double buggy in her direction. Doris crosses over and adjusts the yellow scarf around her neck, which feels a little tight. The mother smiles at her nervously from across the street.

Doris hears her footsteps pounding the pavement towards Lisa's house. She hears in her head different greetings as Twat opens the door. She imagines slapping Twat's face so hard that her face becomes a kind of cartoon version of itself. The thought that people might be 'unfriended' on Facebook is laughable compared to the experience of it in real life. She rehearses what she wants to say to Twat and Cock. How they did something so twisted and so cruel that for a time she stopped believing in the goodness of humankind. How she had thought her life was over, had wanted it to be over, and now she is going to be homeless. The imaginary monologue goes on and on until she knocks and Lisa opens the door and Doris sees that she's heavily pregnant.

***

Tina sees a lunatic running in her direction, screaming and shouting. She's disappointed Doris wasn't at home to look at a few houses together and now this. Tina crosses the street to put distance between them. The lunatic runs past on the other side of the road in a streak of sound and a trail of yellow scarf. Tina recognises the scarf before she processes it; it's Doris, so she turns back the way she came, frightened by the sight of her neighbour. The front door is ajar so she invites herself in. Not again.

They make Doris drink. Guzzle until her stomach is a well, so full it begins to pour over the top and trickle down Utkinton Street, a red rivulet, an S shape all the way to the corner shop and back. They still make her drink, sip it if she has to, faces at the bottom of the glass, she keeps drinking. Swaying and they are still watching. Then it is dark, the colour of a drinker's liver.

This hurt is like a lit cigarette dabbed across the ribs. A grenade in her chest. Cock John and Twat Lisa stir cocktails with the linchpin. She breathes air through a damp handkerchief. Delirious, she lies on the cold tiles; sleep wants to take her.

As her mind swims in and out of consciousness, she sees herself driving, rain glistening on the road and smearing the windscreen. She swerves to miss a cat. John is a backseat driver, throwing commands out of his loose mouth, and Lisa's bound hand and foot in the back of the van with the paintbrushes he's left there after a job. She imagines herself driving to the middle of nowhere. No other cars and no other sound except John asking, asking, 'Where are we? Why are we here? Where are we going?' No one can see them for miles and miles.

Tina can hear Doris sobbing upstairs. She sees the walls in the hall and landing are the colour of a filthy handkerchief. The carpet is so threadbare there is more wood than carpet. There's no hint of Doris's personality to lift the masculine and oppressive gloom and dreariness of the house. It feels and looks exhausted; she wishes Doris could see that for herself.

There is an open tap gushing water in the bathroom, perhaps to drown out her crying. Tina knocks, then waits patiently outside, expecting any minute for Doris to open the door. She does, an hour later.

The stench of acid and vomit is unmistakable. Stinking pink-and-red dribble hangs from Doris's chin, and the yellow scarf is sick-stained. Tina carefully wipes Doris's nose and chin. The bath is so full, it's almost overflowing. There's a razor by the bath, which they both ignore. An ugly, shocking tableau, but Tina has dealt with far worse. She makes Doris put her fingers down her throat until she is purged of the two bottles of wine sloshing inside an empty stomach. The odour is rank, but Tina stays by Doris's side the whole time until the toilet is flushed for the last time. Doris's disastrous marriage is splashed up the walls and over the floor – red red red.

Doris is ashamed that she can't go into work and has to lie to Colleen about having a nasty sickness bug. She wishes she were in the Darwin library now, but she is in no fit state to leave the bedroom let alone the house.

'What the hell were you thinking?' Tina throws the empty wine bottles in the wastepaper bin. An enormous roll of kitchen towel has appeared from somewhere. 'You could lose your job if you carry on like this, and then what? Christ, Doris.'

'Sorry, Tina. I went to see Lisa—'

'What the f—'

'She's pregnant. I don't want to talk about. It. Ever. Can you go?'

Tina flops onto the side of Doris's bed, sympathy in her made-up eyes, the liner as thick as the hard shoulder. She sits on her hair, so she gets up in a panic and rearranges the tresses.

'In that case, I don't blame you! You should have called for me. I've got Prosecco in the fridge.' Tina strokes her friend's matted hair from her face. 'It's gonna get better, I promise.'

Chapter Ten

Andy couldn't park his van in his usual spot outside Winston's home because a highly polished BMW is in it. He is tempted to look under the mat to see if the key is still there but thinks better of it. He knocks and steps inside, conscious of not wanting to appear familiar with the place. The kitchen looks just as it was last time, except for its heart – Winston on his stool.

There is no mistaking the young woman in the photograph with her dark hair and dark eyes. Perhaps now in her early thirties, a successful graduate has gone on to do well for herself, judging by the look of her and her gleaming car. She'd look at home on a horse, he thinks, or in a wine bar with a fifty-pound note in her hand. There's no wedding ring.

Andy takes a moment to remind himself of his role in this meeting: his interest in the mobile home and what remains of the furniture for his mother. But his overwhelming feeling is anger at the sight of the woman standing so close to the window that it seems she would rather be outside than inside, anywhere but here.

Anger has been simmering ever since Winston died; it has kept him awake at night, woken him up with a poke in the ribs, not just the grief but the realisation of the terrible loneliness Winston must have felt. All the time Andy was delivering his food, it had been a social occasion for the old man, a reason to put on a fresh shirt, his leg and his teeth, because no one else visited, no one else seemed to care. Not even his own family, if that's what she is meant to be.

'I'm Katie Howarth. I hear you're interested in buying my dad's place and its contents.' She shakes his hand. Hers is small and soft, and her nails are manicured.

'Mother needs to downsize. Easier if she leaves her furniture where it is. It's not the best. She'll want to know a bit about where she's moving to. Your dad's place, you say?'

'He's just passed away. Look, I haven't got long.'

Katie buttons up her smart wool coat because it's bitterly cold inside the mobile home, seemingly colder than outside. Andy bends down to look at the photographs. Teddy grins at him and he has to fight not to smile back.

'You've had a look round already, I suppose?'

'Another look in the bedrooms would be good.' He waits for her to show him the way and, because he is close at her heels, she has to go inside her dad's bedroom first. By the way she moves, he can sense she doesn't want to. The bed still lacks a mattress.

She flings open the wardrobe like there might be a pleasant surprise in there. 'Have you got a figure in mind, Mr Love?'

Now that she is wedged at the far end of the bedroom and he is by the door, where Winston had sat in his wheelchair that terrible last time, Andy begins. 'Your dad – Winston – died in this room.' Her head jerks back like it's been slapped. 'Right here. I've never seen such a thin man. His ensuite, his bed, the carpet – they were full of shit and vomit. Smelt like it'd been there for days. Days. Like a prisoner. Worse.'

'What—'

'Do you know how he died?' He carries on before she can speak. 'He banged his head picking up Teddy's poo outside. There was a trail of blood all through the house. He was here, bleeding, nothing to eat or drink for days. He said he didn't have anyone to call.' Andy's voice falters. He swallows. 'He said there was no one. But even before that, he'd stopped taking his pills.'

'Get out! Get out now! Who the hell do you think you are to tell me that?'

Andy remains in the same place, his feet rooted to the spot. Unless she climbs onto the bed, she is wedged in the far corner of the room. He knows that in her fancy clothes and high heels she won't do that.

'Your dad loved cake. And Teddy. Your mother, Maureen. And he loved his shirts that used to be in that wardrobe there. What've you done with them?'

Her manicured hands are on her hips. The makeup on her face can't conceal the anger seething behind the lipstick and the eye-shadow. She looks almost ugly now, which makes Andy's job easier.

'The ambulance men said he was alright. But he wasn't. He died a few hours later. Had he been taking his pills? No.' He shakes his head. Remembering that Winston kept his pillbox by his notepad and the address book he sometimes thumbed through, looking for someone to send a birthday card to. 'He'd given up. Not taken a single pill in a week or more.'

'Maybe you should be talking to the ambulance service, not me!'

'You're family. This was neglect. From what I can gather, you were all the family he had after Maureen died. He talked about her all the time. Her laugh. When did you last visit him?'

'What gives you the right—'

'Being the only one for him on his dying day, that's what.'

She stops glancing at her watch, stops taking sharp intakes of breath. He's too big to get past. They both know that. A long sigh oozes out of her mouth and Andy narrows his eyes at her.

'Look, I've been busy. It's—'

'Winston had more self-respect and decency than anyone I know. More good heart than you – you – will ever have.' Andy shakes his head at her, appalled at the very sight of her. 'You call yourself his daughter. What daughter would leave an older man to live alone, to suffer like that, to die alone? He knew you wouldn't give him the time of day in his hour of need, so he gave up. Shame on you! He had one leg, for God's sake.'

'Don't think for one second you can talk to me like that and get away with it! You're a fucking time waster!' Her face contorts into a mask of hate.

Andy exits the bedroom, swipes a couple of photographs of Teddy and Winston and drives away, his heart thumping in his chest. After driving for a few miles, he pulls over to catch his breath. His chest hurts. He can't remember the last time he told someone how he felt.

It is over an hour later when he wakes up and drives the rest of the way home.

***

'Pleased to meet you.' Bosh gives Andy a firm handshake. Andy takes a step back and returns it. 'We're later than we planned because this woman with four kids pushed in front of us in the queue. Didn't she, Jade? I wouldn't have minded if she'd asked, but she didn't, so I told her what I thought about her lack of manners.'

'He did,' Jade nods to reinforce the point, clearly impressed.

The smell of fish and chips is enough to placate Andy. Jade wants to eat in the lounge because her programme's about to start. Louis snuffles at the kitchen door, perturbed not to be invited in. Jade points the remote control like a gun. A shot fires when *The Jeremy Kyle Show* isn't on.

'What?'

Bosh says. 'It's been axed. A guy failed a lie-detector test and later took his own life. It's been all over the papers.'

Jade channel hops and then switches the TV off with a sigh. 'Bosh and I are thinking of getting a tattoo on holiday.'

'What for?'

Bosh says with good humour, 'Self-expression. Like clothes, or blogs – or,' he looks around, 'decor.'

After supper, Bosh heads upstairs to use the bathroom, opens a few wrong doors and then finds the avocado bathroom suite.

'You were a right princess, weren't you?' He takes Jade's hand and kisses it. 'Looks like you didn't want for anything. Who sleeps in there now?' Jade frowns. 'The bed's all messed up.'

Jade glares at him. 'Fish was good tonight.'

It is raining so hard outside they can hear it glugging down gutters and drains and being swilled by tyres driving too quickly. Bosh rummages in a plastic carrier bag and offers Andy a can of lager. Jade is surprised her father accepts and takes it as a sign he likes Bosh. She happily scrolls through the messages on her iPhone. The three of them sip from their cans with the TV on mute. There's a familiar sharp intake of breath from Jade.

'Dad, I don't know whether to show you this or not but – I think you need to see it.'

She reads the messages on Twitter and Facebook. The author is Katie Howarth, and the subject is: #AndyLoveisaPredator

Andy Love is named and shamed as solely interested in verbally attacking a single, grief-stricken woman and meeting her under false pretences. Katie Howarth must have got a look at his van, so Stan's Supermarket is berated for employing the vicious, foul-mouthed man. The verbal abuse goes as far as saying that estate agents should vet people before allowing them into the homes of vulnerable relatives to stop people like Andy preying on the bereft and the fragile, especially women on their own. In capital letters: ANDY LOVE CANNOT BE TRUSTED. She has galvanised support in the shape of likes, followers and comments, including one from Stan which hints at Andy's contract ending abruptly because of his customer-facing role.

'There goes my job,' he says with sad resignation, thinking of his customers who will either think badly of him or miss his friendship. Before Jade and Bosh leave, he explains the truth behind the allegations. They stay longer than planned, thinking they are staying to help him through the shock.

Once they've gone, Andy sits back on the recliner feeling winded. The slandering of his name makes him feel like he's been quarantined in his own home. He walks around the lounge and the kitchen, not quite sure what to do with himself but unable to settle. All those lies and all those people believing them, wanting to stick their beady eyes at a peep-hole into this woman's nasty, made-up world that she's dragged him into. The comments she and others made sound so angry, a feverish kind of frenzy of bad-mouthing, shaming him for being a bully, a predator.

Andy eats half a carrot cake and then finds the shoe polish in the cupboard under the sink because he needs something to do with his hands. He methodically shines the black shoes he usually wears for best occasions like interviews or funerals.

His mobile rings. It's Stan. 'Sorry, mate. I've had cancellations. It's just, once word gets out it spreads like the plague.'

Stifling a carrot-cake burp, Andy says, 'It's all lies, Stan, but I understand your point of view.'

He feels sick for his customers, his friends – especially Margaret, Dave and Gilly. He knows details about their lives that some of their own family members don't.

Forgive Stan for thinking he just knows which brands they like, which special offers appeal. Forgive.

Chapter Eleven

The grandfather clock in the hall chimes nine. There's a smell of polish from the recently polished banister, an elegant dark-wood swirl in a tasteful hall, lit by the light from a stained-glass window to the right of the door.

Colleen cooks and bakes for hours on end, minestrone, cheesy-potato mash, chilli con carne, with Classic FM to keep the silence at bay and a T-towel to warm one shoulder. Afterwards she sits very upright on the sofa, her face lit by the sunshine from the window. It's a warm summer's day outside, which makes her question her choice of recipes. Habit.

Teddy pushes his rear end into her leg, depositing several short, fawn hairs on her nylon tights. She doesn't notice. She doesn't feel. Then he lets out a howl, a long, deep howl, his head tossed back so the sound travels. Colleen sees the pinkness of his tongue and something in her empathises with the sound from his gaping mouth and his sad, deep, dark eyes. It's grief. They need to get out of the house.

In the kitchen drawer, she finds the correct post-it note and leaves its ear under the pepper pot in the kitchen table. The room is immaculate and smells divine. *At the Darwin library.*

She puts Teddy on his lead; he's such a good boy that he walks by her side but it gives her some comfort. She walks the long way to the Darwin, over the Welsh bridge spanning the River Severn where she pauses to watch a rowing boat surge beneath. She feels the warmth of the sun on her face and the cool, rough texture of the stone bridge beneath her hand. It feels like there is more air. She looks at Teddy, wondering if the lightness inside her is down to him.

A vapour trail leaves its mark across the pale blue sky changing the direction of her thoughts to holidays, trips, not necessarily abroad but to Dorset or Yorkshire. Semi-retirement gives her the chance to do these things. No ties now. She shouldn't feel guilty about enjoying herself.

From the bridge, she can see the weeping willows sweeping the surface of the river and the waving tops of chestnut trees. Sunlight shimmers on the water. At the sight of a tramp curled up on a bench, she thinks how lucky she is not to have money worries. Godfrey worked in Lloyds Bank for twenty years and she's enjoyed the same amount of time at the Darwin. The life-insurance policy they took out has been a help to pay off the mortgage. They never wanted children; just the two of them was enough. Over the years she's got a lot of pleasure from reading stories to children, especially the under-fives, typically the same group of children each week. Perhaps she should read *The Water Babies* to them; the underwater world of sharks and eels would fit with their underwater theme.

Walking on the path beside the river, she sees a woman dressed in a yellow polka-dot dress, holding the hand of a little boy. Their colourful clothes mark them out against the homogenous stream of people. The woman looks like Doris and Colleen is about to wave when she looks again and realises it isn't her. She has been so impressed with Doris ever since she started but she is, albeit a cliché, a closed book. Her reference from Clotton Primary School was glowing, confirming what she and Mr Morris had first thought when they met her: *she is an intelligent and capable individual.*

The 'individual' noun in the sentence is the part Colleen finds herself thinking about, and sometimes worrying about, even though she couldn't say having only known Doris as a colleague for six months. For someone who isn't an intellectual snob, Doris resists going into the children's library. It takes her a while to get going some mornings, but when she is in top gear she brings freshness and energy that weren't there before.

Colleen stops at a grocery shop to buy a peach and a dog chew for Teddy. They eat them on one of the benches outside the Darwin, beside his statue and Mary Webb's bust. The gardens are beautiful and immaculate; she makes a mental note to pass comment to Terry from the council. She sits and watches the comings and goings; despite it being a Sunday, the town is busy with shoppers and the like. A gentleman looks at his watch anxiously. A handsome man, mid-fifties, she thinks. He is so smartly dressed and preoccupied with the time that she wonders if he has a date. She smiles at him and he looks away, bashful.

Colleen isn't one for breaking the rules so she justifies unlocking the library on a Sunday by the extra administration she will do once she is inside. The library has the feeling of just being vacated, as though people have slipped out for a quick cup of tea. The desk, which is still her base, is tidy, just as she left it. She leaves her handbag and Teddy's lead there.

They ride in the lift because Teddy's arthritis flares up after a lot of stairs. He doesn't seem to mind the experience and it makes her wonder if he's used to lifts. She should ask Andy next time she sees him. They've been seeing more of each other, which is lovely. One of the nicest places to sit in the library is on a window seat in the old school room, where the thickness of the sandstone walls is exposed. Pity Andy isn't here, she thinks.

As well as making her feel safe, she has a great view of the castle and the irregular shapes of buildings on the skyline, some Tudor, some Victorian. High up on the gothic ceiling are the coats of arms of school trustees. The dark-wood panelling on the wall records the names of scholars who have studied in this very room. GUNT. W.ENGLISH. R.KEATLEY 1840. W.HEPHERD 1871. She can't see Darwin's name, but she knows he was here once.

She listens and hears only her own and Teddy's snuffled breathing amongst the shelves of books and volumes of phrases, words, letters. She loves the fact that the library houses seven thousand books. Some are more than a hundred years old. All that print puts a single existence into perspective.

She runs a finger along the long wooden bench that runs down one wall, along the panelling, along a shelf (local history) to the window seat. The inscriptions of the scholars' names on the panelling are a reminder of mortality – and the potential damage should they be infested with death-watch beetle.

Teddy lowers himself down for a nap while Colleen reads from Margaret Atwood's new novel, a joint Man Booker Prize winner. The sound of a commotion below stops her turning the page. She drops the book and, as quickly as she can, she makes her way downstairs.

The staircase is only lit by emergency lighting. Not for one minute has she considered her vulnerability at being in the library alone without volunteers, Doris, the regulars. A smell of piss hits her first.

Three rogues, one lanky man and two women, pause to look at who is in the building as if she is the one who has gate-crashed their party. Any moment the grimalkin and paddock might appear, and hail, thunder and lightning.

She can hear Teddy's paws awkwardly making their way down the stairs. The witches wait for something to happen.

'The library's closed.' Colleen edges towards the front door. The witches hover by the desk. 'We open again tomorrow.'

The man thrusts something bulky under his grey overcoat and moves towards her. He eyes her up and down very slowly. She feels his eyes undress her and smells his fetid breath. Her bladder feels full; it might leak. The desire to run away is strong.

The woman with a scar through her eyebrow says, 'You work here, don't ya?'

Her friend cackles, spittle flies from her mouth. 'Ya can tell!'

She laughs, making her nose run with snot which she licks away with a blackberry-stained tongue. The man takes charge by moving towards the door. Colleen's knees are shaking.

Teddy finally bounds into the space and barks to try to make an entrance to compensate for his delayed absence. His legs look unstable as he cavorts around. The three witches run through the door, still laughing. Teddy sniffs the air while Colleen quickly locks the door behind them.

She staggers to the desk to put the keys back in her bag but it's gone. Only Teddy's lead is on the desk and an empty bottle of rum. She puts her hands in her hair and wails. A desperate need to urinate sends her running to the toilet.

Chapter Twelve

Adamant.

That was the word Colleen used. She is adamant she is having her party, despite being very shaken by the theft of her handbag from the library. Doris feels pathetic because she is nervous about going to the party and there is Colleen, nearly ten years her senior, soldiering on having experienced a genuine threat to her safety.

Doris owes it to Colleen to take a bath, however much she hates spending time in the bathroom. In the bath, she wishes she could dissolve herself and start again, untouched by a man or a woman. She drinks some of the bathwater to purify her mouth.

Her generous hips are like crags, blotting paper, harsh-sounding consonants, too wide, too protruding for a head to lie across. Is there another half of herself out there? Perhaps moving now behind the frosted glass of the window. Or the half of herself she has lost?

She lathers so much soap on her body that she becomes a soap bubble; one she imagines popping because no one is here to see her laid bare. She misses the touch of skin on skin, the rub of a hand, the touch of a mouth, a breath, moist or dry, something to feel alive. She looks at her hands wrapped around the side of the bath, the skin aged by wrinkles, so terribly soft. She opens her hands in a gesture of openness and abandonment.

The bathroom floor is free from glass, from rolling or shattered wine bottles, not a sign of them with their broken necks spilling blood this way and that where the floor isn't even, seeking a space to dye. Once she liked the honesty of wine in her pores. Its intoxication is inevitable. But the numbness on numbness. Sometimes, she wants to feel.

Still dripping wet, Doris sits in front of her dressing-table mirror to brush her bobbed hair. She looks into her brown button eyes and remembers not just how it feels to be kissed but how it feels to catch a promiscuous glance that says there is the possibility of a kiss. She can't help but focus on the circles under her eyes and her large red mouth.

Not asleep anymore. She could love herself a little bit. The painting of herself. Could she?

The burn on her right hand is still visible after all these years. A silly thing to catch the side of her hand on the roasting dish. Newlywed, she remembers, she was cooking a roast chicken. John gently took her arm and held her hand under the cold water tap, then ever so carefully wrapped it in a bandage. She didn't feel brave at all. She remembers him caressing her cheek, stroking the hair away from her face. Asking, 'Is that better?'

His voice was so full of affection; it *was* better.

She looks at herself close up in the mirror. She feels like a lodger in her own skin. The mirror steams up. Hides her. Good.

She imagines herself driving a yellow Beetle like Tina's, a fake sunflower bobbing on the dashboard, rain glistening on the road and smearing the windscreen. She swerves to miss a cat. John is a backseat driver throwing commands out of his loose mouth, and Lisa's bound hand and foot in the back of the van with the paintbrushes and her jangling bracelets. Doris hears paintbrushes rolling from one side to the other in that tin space; it's a rusty voice of discord from the fine strands of horsehair being whipped from one side to the other as she accelerates around corners. She is dead to Lisa's mouth, and all the colour has gone from her hair, her skin. Lisa is black and white only. She drives her cargo down a dark alleyway and a cobbled street, down a straight fast road, emerging someplace new. She drives to the middle of nowhere because she wants to. No other cars and no other sound, except John asking, asking, where are we? Why are we here? Where are we going? No one can see them for miles and miles.

She hears a dog bark and then a bus trundle by to remind her she doesn't drive. The bathwater is cooling.

You could learn to drive.

Time's running out.

Lisa saw the crow's feet, the frown lines and sagging jaw before she did.

Time's running out.

Not that long ago, Lisa and Doris had prepared dinner together. Lisa chopped lettuce with a sharp blade like it was a machete. Doris made the wine glasses shine before glugging out the red, loving the

70

slosh of liquid against the sides, like a boat without a sail or an oar. The red-haired woman with her was half-dream, half-real, but when their glasses clinked the sound was real enough and so she believed in what she felt.

Over tuna salad, Lisa confessed to the emptiness of her womb which sometimes made her curl up on the floor. They were both in their early forties. Sometime later, Doris quizzed Lisa about how broody she was feeling and Doris thought Lisa must have amnesia by her response.

Doris sees it now in the jaded look on her own face. Time wasn't on their side. Days and decisions got rushed. Hurried. Take away and throw away, until someone got hurt. Lisa was ahead of the game.

Doris brushes her hair, barely seeing herself in the mirror. Was John the one who was used? The keyhole in the door reflected in the mirror has a black face, an ironic curve, a deep hole. Lisa's house is sold. She saw the boards change and the curtains, one by one. Where has she gone to? And John?

Doris quickly blow-dries her hair and dresses, sick of the sight of herself. She tries her knickers on both ways, unsure which way round they go. Typical Mother, making things tricky. She settles for the message *Believe in yourself* at the front where she can see it. She dresses in a cord pinafore and biker boots. She likes colour, so the multi-coloured top adds a splash to her upper body, which she prefers to her legs.

One last look in the mirror. She hides them well, the trembles beneath the pinafore dress. The rehearsal involves creasing her eyes into a smile, a smile like it's been cracked and chipped into her skull. It will be a white-knuckle ride until the booze takes hold, for the routine of drinking wine of an evening (any colour) usually bookends the end of her day. Starting a little earlier won't harm.

She fancies a mug of warm wine because she tried Glühwein once and liked it, so she warms up a mug of red wine in the microwave. It's almost Glühwein but without the cinnamon spice. As the mug is only small, Doris pours the rest of the bottle into a large jug she uses for custard. She's a little afraid her new friend Colleen will turn out like Twat, so she needs a bit of courage.

71

To relax, she sips and reads. Between sipping and turning the page of *To the Lighthouse*, Doris balances her wine glass on a pile of books on her Jenga-style coffee table in the lounge. One of six. Being housebound for months on end, she's read almost a book a day. All those wonderful characters have kept her company: she couldn't possibly give the books away. She alternates the top book depending on her mood or the season. It's *The Testaments* at the moment – an indulgence because it's the hardback, but she feels she owes it to Margaret Atwood.

Doris puts the book down. Her mother is right: she won't be leaving a living legacy behind, not at her age and single. But if she leaves a poem or a short story behind, one that is published or widely read, that moves people, surely that is almost as good as any child legacy? To be published is to be made immortal, arguably better. Not that Doris would dare to take that line of argument with Mother, who thinks she is useless and so is literature. Full stop.

Going to the party might give her ideas and material for characters. Even a good time. The thought spurs her on for an aperitif.

Chapter Thirteen

Westwood is a cul-de-sac of semi-detached bungalows with identical front gardens and internal layouts. All the kitchen windows are above the kitchen sink, looking out of the front of the house. The lounges all have a bay window, which some of the occupants have covered with net curtains or blinds for privacy.

Andy sees Margaret in a white blouse at the kitchen sink. As it's just after eleven o'clock, she's probably washing up her coffee cup and side plate. He hazards a guess it was flapjack – Stan's own from the bakery – one of her favourites. Chocolate-chip flapjack when she feels slim.

Once he parks up, Andy acknowledges with a nod a neighbour who is using a machine to blow leaves into other people's gardens.

'Margaret, it's Andy… Hello!... Margaret, are you there?... It's Andy…'

After knocking, ringing the bell and calling through the letterbox, he has no choice but to leave. It pains him to walk away without the opportunity to explain. He's seen her since she invited him to the cinema and she was fine about that. Now she must believe every word Katie Howarth wrote about him, which means she thinks he's a predator and a bully, a man who can't be trusted, and that's not fine with him.

Andy takes a step back from the door. He sees a shadow pass by the frosted glass. Kneeling, he speaks through the letterbox. 'I know you're in there and I think I know why you're hiding. It's because of that baloney that woman Katie Howarth wrote. It was all lies. But do you know what hurts me most is that you believe what she said about me.'

The letterbox temporarily slams while he takes a breath. There's more. 'I lost my job because of that woman. I found her dad dead. How do you think that was for me? Did you ever think about how I might feel reading what she said about me? Forget it.'

It occurs to him that Gilly and Dave didn't contact him either to see if he was alright after being slandered and dismissed. They can go to

73

hell as well. He slams the letterbox, this time on purpose, and walks briskly towards his van where Louis is waiting patiently for him on the front seat. Louis will be there for him until the day he dies.

He hears Margaret open the front door but he doesn't stop. Life's too short. The man with the blowing machine stares at him.

'Andy!' she shouts. 'Wait!'

'Seize the day!' he shouts back. Through the windscreen, he mouths 'too late' and drives away.

At Colleen's elegant town house, the letterbox opens its mouth to chew on a local paper. Andy pulls it out for Colleen, who has her hands full with the tray. *The Shrewsbury Chronicle*'s headline is *Missing Girl of 13*. Andy hates to think what her parents are going through. From when Jade was thirteen to eighteen, it seemed he barely slept a wink.

He places the paper on the stairs, on top of a pile of freshly-laundered sheets. The smell is comforting, making it harder to follow Colleen into the lounge. He settles into the same chair he sat in last time and readjusts his big feet, so they're pointing away from the bed. He tells her about Margaret and she listens sympathetically then changes the subject to distract him and asks about Jade's new boyfriend.

'He came over on Friday. Bosh.'

'Is this one a keeper?'

'No idea. I can tell Jade likes him, though.'

'How can you tell?'

He says Jade's eyes pass notes to Bosh. The words send a shiver down Colleen's spine. Then he tells her he's lost his job, which makes her gasp, but before she can say anything he says, 'Colleen, I'm having one of those days when you speak your mind. I don't have many.' He takes a deep breath. 'So I'll go for it… Who is the bed for, if you don't mind me asking?'

Andy gestures to the contraption in the window, more medieval rack than comfortable bed. He thinks it's like being in a hospice, only without a sick person and the smell of antiseptic. The shop window for Able World won't do much for Colleen's celebration. He likes Colleen, he likes coming to her house, but the bed is all wrong.

'It was my husband's, Godfrey. I'd rather not talk about it, if you don't mind. It's – it's personal.' Colleen puts her cup and saucer down on the tray and looks out of the partially obscured window. The under-sharing of her generation brings the conversation to a halt.

'Forgive me for asking, but why have it in here?'

'He was in a car crash. It paralysed him. Then he died.'

'I mean, why is it still in here ... now he's not?' Andy asks tenderly. He tries to read Colleen's expression. She sits very still like she is waiting for something to crash through the window at any minute. 'You're having a party later. I'm in my van. Maybe it's a good time to—'

Andy drains his cup dry and loads up the tea tray with the dirty crockery. Colleen is still in the lounge by the time he's washed, dried up and questioned his decision to tackle the subject several times over.

Only the physical space of the hall divides them but Colleen takes herself very far away, into herself, the burden of guilt overshadowing the remnants of grief she hadn't allowed herself to feel yet. She rubs her hands up and down her lap, once, twice, three times. If she closes her eyes and then re-opens them, perhaps she'll know what to do. Her eyes flicker behind the lids, little searching movements, circles, she imagines.

Godfrey played beautiful music and he wrote lyrics. She's kept his music in the piano stool. Wouldn't it be better to remember him through the good things he left behind? Perhaps she could learn to play. Wouldn't that be better to remember him by rather than the steel bars to stop a grown man from falling out of his bed?

She puts her head in her hands. If only he hadn't driven to the garage for a paper. He could have walked in almost the same time it took him to drive. Hours and hours longer in the end, by the time they'd cut him out of the Citroën.

'Shall I be off then?' Andy stuffs his hands in his pockets.

The door to the music room is ajar; inside, there's a symphony of illness and death. If only I could be held by Andy right now, she thinks, but at least she's known how wonderful that can feel and that's more than some have.

Another chime from the grandfather clock. Colleen takes a large intake of breath before standing bolt upright. Her posture is always excellent. 'You're right. You're right. Let's clear it now while I can— while we can—'

They clear the lounge and music room within the hour. If Colleen notices the curtain-twitching and freeze-frames on the pavement, she doesn't show it. Andy has no idea where to go with so much equipment in his van, but he'll work it out. Later he reflects on the satisfaction on her face when he closed the van door on all the memories inside. She wore a wholesome expression, like a face after a satisfying meal, a few quid well spent, a book with a conclusion that both ends and lingers.

Colleen's cheeks are glowing with the effort and sheer relief when she waves him off. His van indicates for a time before he can pull out onto the street. He's conscious of the ticking sound of the indicator because she's watching, but when he looks at her in his rear-view mirror he sees her simply smiling, because the naked eye can't see the synapses reshaping in her brain or the muscle fibres loosening in her neck and shoulders. He can't see it but she can feel it, and it feels wonderful.

Andy feels good about himself all the way home. He's looking forward to celebrating Colleen's semi-retirement party later at her house with her friends. At home, he looks at his face in the bathroom mirror and sees beard. Not much else. He scratches it. Before Catherine, he was always clean-shaven and enjoyed splashing on a bit of aftershave – Brut, or Blue Denim. Catherine used to buy him Aramis at Christmas time. She kissed him more when he smelt good.

'It's time,' he says to his reflection.

Otis Redding's voice and Louis accompany Andy upstairs to the bathroom. He starts on the right-hand side, first with scissors then his razor. The face in the mirror is a weird profile kind of face, a Jekyll-and-Hyde face. His mouth twitches and wiggles with its newly found freedom. He runs a hand across the right cheek and enjoys its silky touch. Then he mirrors his actions on the left side. When it's done, he pulls the plug and watches years of himself flush away. It's a slow kind of whirlpool of hair and water and grubbiness; the speed gathers until there is very little of it left. He feels a bit naked but in a good way.

***

Doris has to look twice at the woman who opens the front door to a smart town house opposite the abbey. A very glamorous and sophisticated Colleen. She has never seen her look so young and so transformed. 'You look like a film star!' says Doris

Doris makes all the right noises in Colleen's spotless kitchen. The matching kettle and toaster, the enormous kitchen clock and wonderful oak bookcase full of books. Not just cookery books (of which there are several) but fiction, poetry, plays. A mini-library. Doris would happily browse the shelves for the rest of the evening but she has enough social awareness to know that would be rude.

Colleen cajoles her into the lounge once Doris has parted with three bottles of wine, one of each hue. A large man is snuggled into a wing-back chair, singing along to a track by Aretha Franklin playing low from a speaker in the room. He looks like a cherub. Doris likes the way he occasionally sips from a handled pint glass in the pauses, showing more self-restraint in the face of alcohol than she's ever shown. The lounge is a soaring kingfisher blue, which looks kindly on complexions.

Colleen sashays in carrying a platter of canapés and tiny crustless sandwiches, her earrings swinging. Doris generally eats hotdogs or sweets so declines, but she enjoys watching other people eat them

'Finger food!' exclaims Andy, always enthusiastic about food. He sits more upright in his chair in anticipation and takes a serviette and several canapés at once without self-consciousness.

'They are canapés, not finger-food!' says Colleen, feigning haughtiness. 'Andy, this is Doris; Doris, this is my friend Andy. He's a regular in the audiobook aisle.'

'Bit small,' he swallows one whole. 'But tasty. Hi, Doris. Don't mind Louis.' The salty canapé slips into Andy's mouth like an eel through the water.

Doris pats Louis's head and, by the way he pushes his rear end into her leg, decides he likes her. She looks abashed while Teddy sits beside him, feeling left out of the attention. They chat about Darwin Library, books they have read or plan to read and the tasteful décor in Colleen's house. Suddenly, out of context, Doris says, 'I need rehoming,' and laughs nervously.

Colleen looks at Andy, unsure what to say.

'Separation. My other half owns the house. I suppose divorce is next. I'm new to—'

'Would you like a glass of lemonade?' asks Colleen but Doris shakes her head. 'I'll get you some peanuts. You're not allergic, are you?'

Between Colleen's earrings are her nails. Eye-bright purple, flawless, enough to worship, a fairy tale. Doris's half-moons, jagged tales, fragments of tissues she's wiped her eyes with and dropped down her fingernail.

'How do you make your nails look so pretty, Colleen?' she asks, eyeing up her own chapped hands and pasty nails, her hand shaking. 'Mine are full of white bits like a shaken snow globe.'

'Not enough calcium,' Andy says. 'Jade, my daughter, was the same. Had to buy strawberry flavouring to add to full-fat milk. Can't tell you what her nails are like now because they're always blue or glittery.'

Andy chats away to Doris, whom he likes immediately. She likes him because he tries to put her at ease and talk to her, even though she's a bit off and a bit drunk. They talk about insomnia, more common than they all thought. Colleen tells them she once nodded off in the doctor's surgery while waiting to see her doctor about the very same problem. When Andy said there's always an upside, which is the birds, the women in the room longed to be looked at. Doris thought of the moon but felt too shy to talk about it.

It is eleven o'clock and Doris has awful hiccups. She usually feels self-conscious about her generous hips as people look thin, tall, elegant, but these few new friends – sapling friendships in an orchard of sorts – there's real sap oozing ever so silently when they talk. Doris likes looking at the face in the armchair; she feels at home there, on the bridge of his nose, the space between his eyes. Andy drinks Guinness, anthracite in a glass. She notices his broad sloping shoulders judder up and down when he laughs at a joke, or is it because of her hiccups? His name registers in her brain, a new memory hopefully pushing out an old one.

The room is spinning for Doris. Some of Colleen's female friends look more and more friendly, fish-like with their pouty mouths in shimmering lipstick. A lady with a glass of white wine has her back to her: the leather trousers look a trifle tight around the crotch. Her name is Alice and she has a pension and a budgie. Is there a connection?

Cruises are talked about with some interest. It becomes clear to Andy and Doris that there are some wealthy, well-travelled people in the room, people from a time when Colleen and her deceased husband rubbed shoulders with 'a set'. Doris talks about a time she and John went wild swimming in a lake in France, the water a perfect temperature and feeling as alive as they ever felt. Andy volunteers a description of a holiday with Jade in a caravan in Anglesey when she was twelve. He smiles lopsidedly at the memory; that's all the women can tell you.

Doris's mouth is working non-stop because ideas are firing at an astonishing rate, and people are listening. She tells them she wants to write something good, so good it could be on a shelf in the Darwin. How it must feel to open the cave of a mouth after dormancy so upturned that bats, once resident takes rapid flight, turning the sky black with wings. She says she wants wings for her words so they can fly straight into people's ears and disintegrate in their minds.

Colleen tucks Doris up for a little nap in her bedroom because the bed is aired, unlike the others. She switches on the sidelight in case Doris falls asleep and wakes up wondering where she is. The glass of water beside her is untouched. Colleen wonders about adding a splash of blackcurrant to dupe Doris into drinking it.

'Does he see my red?' Doris slurs. 'My house is red, but he doesn't know that it's patterned with congealment, the haemorrhaging...' hiccup '...of a marriage, a miscarriage, blood from floor to ceiling. Lisa...' hiccup ' ...is he free of gashes?'

Colleen strokes her clammy hand, tempted to ask who she's referring to, but thinks better of it. It is Colleen's first party, a first stab at entertaining since Godfrey died, and she has loved every moment. At last it feels like Godfrey is under his gravestone and she allows herself to enjoy a new day without guilt or shame. She tiptoes out of the room, assuming Doris is asleep.

Doris counts to one hundred, drinks the glass of water in one go, and heads straight through the front door, unable to climb the necessary stairs into a conversation with someone downstairs. She is determined not to lose her job for being pissed at a colleague's party. As she closes the front door, she wishes she was extraordinary, bold, sober. She is none of these things and so runs all the way home to a known world. The party has been a prism, a wonderful prism.

Chapter Fourteen

The letter from the estate agents says she will need to vacate 42 Utkinton Road by 31st October or face eviction. The impersonal letter, which will turn her life upside down on Halloween, trembles in her hands. She is going to be homeless if she doesn't act quickly. Eviction. Tough talk, not celebrity eviction talk like Davina sprouts on *Big Brother*. Real.

He makes her drink. Guzzle until her stomach is a well, so full it begins to pour over the top and trickle down Utkinton Street, a red rivulet, an s shape all the way to the corner shop and back. He still makes her drink, sip it if she has to, his face at the bottom of the glass, she keeps drinking. Swaying and he is still watching. Then it is dark, the colour of a drinker's liver.

A grenade in her chest. Cock John and Twat Lisa stir cocktails with the linchpin. She breathes air through a damp handkerchief. Delirious, she lies on the cold tiles; sleep wants to take her.

As her mind swims in and out of consciousness, she sees herself driving, rain glistening on the road and smearing the windscreen. She swerves to miss a cat. John is a backseat driver, throwing commands out of his loose mouth, and Lisa's bound hand and foot in the back of the van with the paintbrushes he's left there after a job. She imagines herself driving to the middle of nowhere. No other cars and no other sound except John asking, asking, 'Where are we? Why are we here? Where are we going?' No one can see them for miles and miles.

Doris washes and dresses. Enough of daydreaming about action, revenge, being someone she's not. She has to do something to move out of the ever-decreasing space in her head. *Ruminating*. That is the word the doctor uses.

The consulting room is familiar to her; this is her tenth visit in as many months. It is a Monday morning and the waiting room is full. Doris always gets the first appointment so she can avoid being looked at by other sick people. She's read everything there is to read in the waiting room. She removes her yellow scarf because it's a bit stuffy in Dr Timpson's consulting room and last time he felt the glands in her neck.

The check-up always starts with the same open question. 'How have you been feeling, Doris?'

It's like the endless splattering of waves up the stroke side and bow side of an idle rowing boat. Slap. Slap. Slap. The murky water slaps at the bow as if it were a face. A tireless slapping, one after the other. Like an assault with no retaliation. The wind is passive and there are no oars, no cox, so I am marooned, stranded with myself, unable to escape myself and the slap, slap, slap.

And the wet slapping sound haunts my waking moments and my dreams. It spreads like damp, from the floorboards up through the walls of my skin, till it discolours my outlook: everything I see, everything I do, everything I hear. Everything even smells a bit damp, a bit off, musty. Rotting. Even memories discolour. Once the damp is in my brain, each thought is imperfect, a little injured, frayed in some way.

A two-headed monster doesn't pop out because it's already inside me. If only something tangible would appear to ratify my illness! Even when the water's calm, I sense turmoil is coming. And so it does. There are no answers, just questions; no ropes for rationality, only knots of confused, distressing thoughts.

My brain now sounds like a three year old's because it asks the same questions over and over and over again. The loop must take parents close to insanity. It ends with sleep, the dead kind, not leaving a refreshed breezy feeling, more like being roused from the dead. Then the loop starts again.

Every sound, scent, touch, is blunt. Boiled. Life's a black-and-white film on mute. It seems like I have no taste buds, I leave no fingerprints, I have no edge. I've become an abstract painting of fading shades of black, grey, stone.

Of course, she always says the same thing: 'Fine. I'm almost out of anti-depressants.'

Another month and, if there's no improvement, Dr Timpson suggests she starts another course of anti-depressants with a stronger dose. She must try to think of her depression as any other illness which needs treatment. Her sense of failure because she is taking drugs for her illness is therefore unfounded. She is sceptical of his wisdom because he also says eating a banana every day will lift her mood. A banana?

Doris is glad of the umbrella, though its handle is rough and charred from the funeral pyre. On days like these it would be convenient to drive, not just because of the miserable weather but to do a simple drive-by; not to stop and get out of the car but to turn one's head to the side and look for as long as the drive-by allows. Seconds, but enough.

She wants to know if they are still living in Lisa's house or whether Lisa's brother has won his battle and got the place sold and kicked them out. It is a more saleable proposition than John's place, having been beautifully decorated and carpeted. Lisa has quite a flair for interior décor. She chose a theme for each room. Her bedroom theme is purple; the bathroom the beach.

If Doris comes face to face with them, she has prepared a little speech; Alexa has heard it many times. But the pavement is bare. She can see the sign before reaching Lisa's house protruding above the front door like a rigid sail. It is in the hands of the same estate agent as her place but this one is SOLD.

The road has an unusual name for a row of very ordinary terraced houses, unremarkable in every way except for Lisa's red door. Barbados Street. Red. Doris's breathing becomes shallow as she walks by the red front door and then the lounge window.

She peers inside – to catch a glimpse of emptiness. The room is bare. Bankrupt of people and things, of blazing red hair, of floral cushions on the sofa, of a soft wool throw Lisa used to hang over one arm of the sofa. Lisa's mother spent a lot of time watching television and had paid for Sky and Netflix. When she passed away, Lisa said her mother had paid for an annual subscription until September, so she might as well enjoy the choice while she could afford it. Around this time last year, Doris and Lisa had settled on the sofa side by side with a bottle of plonk and a box of Maltesers and watched *Fleabag* from start to finish, twice. When Doris got home, she'd found stray long red hairs on her cardigan. She'd peeled them off carefully and studied them in the light.

A surge of emotion catches her off guard. All these months she's feared she might bump into them, has loathed the proximity of them, but now… Where are they? Are they all right? Has Lisa given birth to a healthy baby? Does it look like John or Lisa?

Doormat.

A car drives past too quickly, splashing water from the gutter. The radio is so loud in the car that Doris can name the track: *Material Girl.* It turns off Barbados Street, leading to a new, small estate. Hollow Green. It sounds like an oxymoron to her but it looks like a sweet place to live.

Why must she have answers? The teacher at the front of a class used to throw out a question and scan for a raised hand at Cotton Primary School where Doris worked. When not a single limb reached upwards, the teacher Doris supported – Mr Keating – would ask a poor child directly in an accusatory manner. If Doris was sitting next to them, sometimes she felt a rise in their temperature or a stirring motion on the plastic chair that made her feel sorry for them.

Doris has questions. When did the affair start? Do they love each other? What's the sex like? Do they talk about her?

Doormat.

She stops her thoughts in their tracks and walks briskly home. Home. That temporary residence of hers she is 'borrowing' from her estranged, cheating husband who is selling it from under her feet. The rain thuds on the umbrella rhythmically, quicker than her footsteps which work at an even, steady pace. The raindrops are like shrapnel and rebound off the pavement, soaking her black leggings.

By the time she walks through the front door, she is cold and sodden but her headache has subsided thanks to the fresh air — every cloud. Dr Timpson says to appreciate the good things, however small.

Doris recognises her mother's handwriting on the envelope face up on the hall mat. She has come good: inside a small parcel is a cheque for £9,000, another packet of knickers in various hues with the words *Believe in yourself* emblazoned on the front, and a short note.

Dear Doris,
Find somewhere nice to live with a spare room.
Love Mum

It is a genie out of a bottle. This feeling is what Dr Timpson meant by a happy chemical. The kindest thing her mum has done for her in a very long time. Doris hasn't realised how much she missed seeing her mother's handwriting. Did she walk to the post box in a headscarf to post it herself? The image puts a smile on Doris's face. The determined, gritty way her mother takes on the simple task of putting one foot in front of the other. She has been in her mother's thoughts, though why she specifies Doris needs a spare room she's not sure. Or what, if any, the connection is with new knickers.

The wet umbrella leans against the fridge, dripping onto the linoleum floor as Doris prepares a round of toast coated in chocolate spread, smiling as she spreads.

Before Doris's father disappeared, Mother dressed in bright clothes to express her joy in life. Her hair was curled at the ends into a perfect kink around her head. Doris was eleven when Mother converted into a depressed nun, angry with everything and everyone, shuffling around in her slippers as if it were too much trouble to lift her feet properly, let alone curl her hair.

Her mother could be as fierce as a bull to anyone who crossed their path, so Doris didn't tell her about Caitlin's daily bullying in the lunch hour, or the boys who made fun of her flat chest, or missing her dad, or the mockery at her ineptitude on sports day. By the end of adolescence, she was fit to burst. She got through college and socialising by drinking at home before she mixed with people; it took the edge of her shyness, helped her giggle in the right places.

Once Mother took up painting, she came back to life. Something in the smell of oils and turps, in the sound of strokes on canvas, the scraping of a palette knife, soothed her creased disposition. She painted faces from books, magazines, no one she knew, which Doris always found strange. Then, once, she painted Doris.

Doris often regretted sitting for her mother a few years after she'd married John. Once she saw herself through the eyes of her mother, she took so many steps backwards that there was always a distance between them that she hadn't yet overcome. The figure of herself was small in a large canvas, dominated by abstract shapes and bold patterns, a nothingness, it seemed to her. The only detail in Doris's figure that was significant was her frightened eyes. Even the posture of her shoulders suggested defeat. She saw a face she wouldn't hang on her wall for love or money because it was a plain, weak face. It said to Doris her mother didn't love her.

If only to be loved, or at least to be alive in someone else's head. Was that what she missed since Cock and Twat ran out of her life? To be resident, however briefly, is a kind of affirmation of existence. But why does she need others to affirm her? If her child hadn't poured out of her body onto the bathroom floor, she would have been an affirmation. The best kind. But she isn't coming back. The doctor has helped her see that. He told her she could make a difference to her mental health and wellbeing by the way she interpreted events. The subject of her miscarriage could not be included in that little nugget of wisdom, surely?

Doris retraces her steps under the wet umbrella. She has to act now; it feels like if she doesn't, she won't be able to ever again. Acting is a good thing. This trip to Lisa's house is about her taking control of her thoughts. Dr Timpson would be pleased if he knew what she was doing. After all, to scroll through houses on Right Move is the one thing she's done without anxiety because it is a virtual world; she is just a voyeur fingering a mouse. This is real life.

At one end of Hollow Green, they've built six identical semi-detached houses, each with a porch and a front and back garden, parking but no garage. The rest of the estate is given over to detached properties of various sizes out of Doris's price range. The turf at the front of each house is freshly laid and the brightest green she has seen in a while. It's a small development, with numbers only climbing up to the twenties. The name of the estate has come because of the developers' wisdom; they punched a hole through the fences running at the back of the houses so hedgehogs can move freely, and from the bird boxes on the house and under the eaves. After decimating a green field teeming with wildlife in a suburb of Shrewsbury, it is the least they could do.

In the show house, the brand-new kitchen and bathroom sparkle and the smell of new carpets is unmistakable. A dishwasher, electric oven, all new. In the master bedroom, Doris looks at herself in the mirrored fitted wardrobe. She looks taller, thinner. She slowly wanders into each room, enjoying the neutral colour scheme, the perfectly smooth walls and the colourful wallpaper on statement walls – no signs of decay. A brand-new house is like a blank page, each room a chapter waiting to be written. No one has died here; no one has been born here. No one knows the middle or the ending; living in this house could be her story.

Back at the shabby residence on Utkinton Street, she appraises its contents with a fresh pair of eyes. It is odd, like she's wearing glasses or has taken off a pair that were too strong. Should she take the familiar sofa with her to her new abode on Hollow Green? It has a superb memory of the bottoms that have sagged on it over the years. It's a sloppy kind of sofa, the cushions have lost their collagen, the elasticity of the seating experience is almost over – but it knows her body.

She picks up things, puts them down again. There's a kind of vulture activity at large, picking over what's left of the carcass John and Lisa killed: the marital home, well used, once well-loved. It is the terror of a new life, of living, not dying, of moving to a new web, of regaining and losing memories, of waking up to be a new person, different nerves and incisions – it's all that and more that frightens her. If only she were brave and competent like Colleen.

She begins to sort frantically through the contents in a teak chest of drawers in the lounge – one pile to keep, the other to discard. The acid taste of betrayal returns to her mouth. How can she put the bitterness she feels in the discard pile? It must not be packed away to go with her because it will sour her new start.

A very short story of hers pokes out from the discard pile, crumpled but hers. Doris wrote it when she was at secondary school during her Stephen King phase of experimenting with horror and elements of science-fiction. The story is called *My Father, the Serial Killer* and at the bottom of the page in her mother's unmistakable handwriting it says *A++++ you are brilliant my little Doris*. The story is based around the theme of 'be careful what you wish for', illustrated by the return of a violent father to a small family in Cumbria who wind up dead.

***

Her offer on 12 Hollow Green is accepted and the process to move in within six weeks is in motion, leaving only a week between her leaving 42 Utkinton Street and John, or whoever, moving in. The deadlines are written across her brow in frown lines, but without one she might not act. Her mother is delighted with Doris's decision to buy a new house. She says the knickers must have done the trick and cackled.

Doris looks at the objects in the lounge window facing Utkinton Street, a quiet and familiar road. The postcard has faded in the sun. The ice-cream box is empty but still in place, and the avocado stone is rotting. She throws the items in a plastic bag and places the brochure for Hollow Green in the centre. Her page is updated and shared. She walks around the house, itemising what goes, what stays.

What did Lisa say sorry for? For stealing John? For betraying their friendship? Or something else? She decides to leave the sorry double bed. Even if it wasn't treacherous, the possibility is there. It can stay.

Chapter Fifteen

Colleen stirs in her sleep then wakes up suddenly, sensing something or someone is in the bedroom with her. The ethereal sense that comes after a vivid dream still lingers. Godfrey was talking to her from his bed, the top half of him shamelessly looked normal, firm. The white cover hid the bottom half, where the muscles in his legs had once been, before jaws had shaken them like a teddy and torn the seam, expelling stuffing and sinew.

Her mouth feels dry. She blinks to shake the lingering ill-at-ease feeling but it doesn't pass. The rational part of her brain doesn't believe in ghosts but the other half, the one sensing something in the room with her this very moment, isn't so sure.

Her hands tremble as she pushes herself upright. Unsure whether to switch the light on or not, she strains her eyes at the faint outline she thinks she sees at her dressing table. The grogginess has passed now: her senses are firing. A glass perfume bottle topples over and something small rolls off onto the carpet.

'Who's there?'

Colleen's shaking hand reaches for the sidelight. The switch makes a loud clicking sound and then the room is bathed in light, but it is the sounds from downstairs that startle her out of bed. Her floral nightdress falls to her feet as she climbs out and grabs her dressing gown from the ottoman.

'Is someone down there?'

Breaking glass answers her question – then the dull sound of wood, the thud of objects landing from a height. A wave of sickness passes through her. She looks for a heavy object to carry but can only find a volume of Ted Hughes' poetry. From the top of the stairs, she flicks the landing and hall lights on and gasps.

Forgetting herself, she runs down the stairs and hops between the debris on the hall floor. Teddy is barking from somewhere: she can't place where, though. The black-and-white tiles are partially obscured by coats, a bag and broken ornaments.

She recognises the man from his grey overcoat. He is in the lounge, opening drawers, rifling through papers; the two women rush past loaded with clothes and bags taken from the hall, wearing jewellery they must have stolen from upstairs.

'Get out of my house!' Colleen yells and reaches for the phone in the hall. It occurs to her that Teddy is trapped in the understairs cupboard. His barks continue, muffled and frustrated.

'No, you don't.' The man in the overcoat pushes Colleen over. The phone hits the floor, the dead tone in their ears. She lands awkwardly on her side, cries out, feels like something has snapped, broken. From her view from the ground, she sees debris on the kitchen floor, cupboards ajar. A cookery book is open on the kitchen floor, open at a dessert page. Profiteroles, she thinks.

'Where's ya money?' the man says, standing over her like a portent.

Colleen starts to cry. A trickle of wee runs down her leg. 'My handbag. In there.' She gestures to the music room.

The two women fly in and hastily out again with Colleen's handbag in hand.

She hears them empty the contents on the carpet. She is shaking uncontrollably now. Swimming in and out of consciousness, she hears tuneless notes banged on the piano, the clinking of her crystal decanter and glasses being bagged, and then nothing.

It is morning when she comes to; she can hear the birds singing and a wand of light is shining through the stained glass in the front door window. She knows they have gone because, apart from the silence, there isn't the stench of piss and booze.

Sounds of footsteps and laughter on the other side of the door send her heart rate rocketing. Can she get up from the floor? The defeated part of her is happy to stay there. But they have a key and any minute they might decide to return. If she stays on the floor, she will save the man the trouble of pushing her over again.

Anger gets her up, anger with herself for stupidly going to the library on a Sunday and leaving the doors unlocked and her handbag on the library desk. Even if they hadn't followed her home, there were probably enough details in the bag to give away her address. Stupidly she'd thought that was the end of it once she'd put a stop to her cards and her phone.

Colleen shuffles over to the banister and wraps her arms around it. A rib or two feel broken. Teddy is panting and dribbling when she manages to let him out of the cupboard.

Bit by bit, she gets to her unsteady legs. Blood from her cuts has dried on her Laura Ashley dressing gown. She catches sight of her face in the hall mirror and looks away. She puts the latch on the front door and walks into the lounge, her hands pressed against the wall to steady herself. The curtains are still drawn and she is glad, because the darkness partly conceals the damage. The banging in her head is incessant. She closes her eyes and, sometime later, falls asleep.

The shame of having her private life rifled through makes her sob uncontrollably. Just the sight of her post-it notes on the floor and kitchen counter make her feel exposed and weak. They had eaten and drunk in her kitchen, probably while laughing at her shopping lists, the cards she'd kept from friends, prayers, the calendar listing people's birthdays and trips out. Right now, the packet of gold serviettes tossed on the kitchen floor belong to another universe. A large bite has been taken out of a slab of cheddar under the cloche, which is shipwrecked on its side. The alphabetised bookshelves have gaps where there weren't any before.

Their complete disregard for her as a fellow human being brings her to her knees. They have no respect. Not animals. Not anything. The violation she feels makes her dizzy.

She bolts the kitchen door and then frets that they might still be upstairs but she doesn't have the strength to go up there. No doubt they will have rummaged through her underwear drawer, and she knows they've taken jewellery from her bedroom. She listens intently but all she can hear is blood rushing in her ears. What day is it? Judging by the sounds of traffic and footfall outside, she thinks it's a weekday. How long has she been passed out? It could be Monday or Tuesday, in which case she should be at work. But there is no way she can face going outside and seeing people. She can't even bring herself to look at her own face in the mirror.

The grandfather clock chimes. It's eleven o'clock. The library will be staffed. She rehearses what she wants to say, takes a deep breath and delivers a lie. Usually she avoids lying at all costs but she deems it necessary on this occasion. She says she has a terrible cold and won't be in work this week.

Frederick is very sympathetic because he knows Colleen rarely takes a day off work. His cheery, friendly voice sounds very far away; it has a tinge of lanterns of blossom and summer trees flaunting their leaves in a distant land that she fears she might not have the courage to see again.

Chapter Sixteen

Although he's only been on a few dates with Doris since Colleen's party, Andy finds himself thinking about her a lot of the time. Odd little things, really, like the smallness of her hands, and the hair clips she liked to wear and her lemony smell.

She didn't like the romcom they went to see at the Odeon cinema but they had a good chat afterwards, sharing a bag of pick'n'mix, and then a few days later a nice afternoon in a few second-hand bookshops in Much Wenlock. She'd chosen two audiobooks for him in the Darwin which had been right up his street, but he's tried to not visit the library too often for fear of frightening her away. He hasn't met anyone as curious as Doris; she seems to see things differently to other people. He's been looking forward to seeing her on Sunday and has gone to some trouble to look smart – but not obviously so.

His hi-vis jacket is hung on a peg in the hall. His workmen's boots are out of sight under the kitchen table. The keys to his customised van are in the kitchen on a peg by the fridge. He and Louis go for a walk and sit in the bandstand in the middle of the Quarry Park, looking for her figure to appear on the path around the perimeter. It is a breezy day for August, bringing out woolly hats and the odd scarf. He self-consciously strokes his belly then glances at his watch.

He's described the bandstand to Doris in minute detail; he knows the features like his face. They were in the café drinking mugs of steaming tea when he told her how much he likes this spot so she'd wanted to see it with him: he wanted her to visualise the place, the avenue of sycamore and oak trees, the flow of the river to some place the path doesn't mind; the cut grass emerald green. He's described the iron bridge straddling the River Seven, a thick girth at this point in its journey to the sea.

Andy didn't notice a shadow pass across her face when he affectionately described the games children play with balls, kites and scooters, or the mums who run with prams along the smooth path. He said it was a romantic place to the hallowed person beside him – not knowing her at all.

He shuffles his feet, wishing they were warm in his boots. The hard seat in the bandstand is turning his bottom numb. He lets Louis off the lead so he can bound around with the other dogs. It gives him something new to watch. Later, Louis follows him over the bridge where Andy pauses halfway across and looks down into the fast-flowing river where a brace of ducks are making their journey beneath him.

He'd offered to sit in on a few driving lessons but Doris had shaken her head vehemently at that. Andy can't imagine his life without a vehicle in it. He'd shared his dream of driving down Route 66.

Louis frolics on ahead, happy to be heading to an open-air cafe. Andy orders a coffee and a bacon sandwich that he barely knows he's eating.

They rarely have much to say to each other but to him that doesn't matter. Andy likes that Doris only speaks when she has something meaningful to say. He likes their silences as much as their conversations.

She isn't coming. He's seen the best and worst of the afternoon; he strolls home with Louis on the lead so he doesn't feel quite so alone. At the corner shop he buys *The Shropshire Star*, a Mars Bar and a king-size Twix to eat on the way home. On page three, an article describes the suicide of Mr Dave Rode, his once-friend and once-customer, a recluse age thirty-one, from Curfew Terrace. So Stan lost Dave's business anyway.

***

He makes her drink. Guzzle until her stomach is a well, so full it begins to pour over the top and trickle down Utkinton Street, a red rivulet, an S shape all the way to the corner shop and back. He still makes her drink, sip it if she has to, his face at the bottom of the glass. She keeps drinking. Swaying and he is still watching. Then it is dark, the colour of a drinker's liver.

A grenade in her chest. Cock John and Twat Lisa stir cocktails with the linchpin. She breathes air through a damp handkerchief. Delirious, she lies on the cold tiles; sleep wants to take her.

As her mind swims in and out of consciousness, she sees herself driving, rain glistening on the road and smearing the windscreen. She swerves to miss a cat. John is a backseat driver, throwing commands out of his loose mouth, and Lisa's bound hand and foot in the back of the van with the paintbrushes he's left there after a job. She imagines herself driving to the middle of nowhere. No other cars and no other sound except John asking, asking, 'Where are we? Why are we here? Where are we going?' No one can see them for miles and miles.

She imagines Cock and Twat pushing a black pram under the canopies of oak trees so thick the sun is shaded away from their faces. Beneath the trees they pause to look at the River Severn, the bandstand, the mown grass. Their child is too young to throw food for the ducks but next year she will be big enough.

'Sorry, Andy,' she slurs from the view of the bathroom floor.

***

Andy undresses in Jade's old bedroom. Louis prefers to sleep on the landing on these occasions. The bedsheet feels damp and cold beneath him; he usually sleeps on top of the duvet but it's heading into autumn now and he's got cold in the park, so he feels the need for covers and warmth.

Jade loved her bedroom and so did her friends, especially the unicorn duvet and the pink-feather bows around the heart-shaped mirror. The posters of boy-band members are still in the same place, though they won't be boys anymore. Andy switches off the Thumbelina night lamp and falls straight to sleep.

Chapter Seventeen

Doris stares at the unopened bottle of wine that is temporarily residing by the toaster. After seeing Andy and apologising for standing him up, she was shocked he was so hurt and upset. He's started growing a beard, which has put years on him. She shakes her head, ashamed at herself for hurting someone. Of all people, she should know better.

The glass bottle is shapely, the hip that takes the bottom to the neck especially. She pours herself a large glass. Frees it from standing by the mundanity of the toaster.

Just one.

Colleen is still off work so Doris told Andy about the job driving the library bus that is called Babs and travels around Shropshire and stops at designated spots and times. It is an invaluable service to customers who are unable to get into the town. She gave him an application form and printed off the details, even though he didn't seem interested. He barely looked at it, stuffed it in his coat, a plain navy one. She misses his hi-vis jacket. She said sorry again.

Just two.

Andy hasn't heard from Colleen either. Doris left a message last week but still hasn't heard back. Not like Colleen at all. The new art exhibition on the top floor of the library is proving popular – a local artist. Nice chap. Likes reading Robert Macfarlane. She hopes Colleen will approve of what's she done with the space and the promotional activity to underpin its success. Sam's mum has been in, asking for Teddy. And the reading group loved Helen Dunmore. Doris rings Colleen again. No answer.

Doris stands up from the kitchen table to top up her glass but something about Colleen's prolonged absence and lack of communication stops her. She grabs her coat, scarf and a torch and sets off on the long walk to her house. Exercise is good for her, and daily acts of kindness. To add a third big tick to the list supplied by dear Dr Timpson, on the way she eats a banana that is very ripe having sat in the bottom of her bag for some time. She waits for her mood to lift like magic.

Outside Colleen's house, she's relieved to see sidelights on behind the curtains like modest halos. Doris stamps her feet to keep warm while she waits to be let inside. It takes a long time for Colleen to unlock and open the door. Doris has come to the window first to show her face. It reminds her of the garage she sometimes calls at late at night for a top-up; after eleven o'clock, the money is exchanged through a kind of hatch. It makes her feel like a prisoner with an alcohol addiction.

It is as if her purple nail varnish has wiped itself across Colleen's face, around her eyes especially, changing them into great thunderclouds ready to explode with a downpour of blood. One lip is puffy and enlarged like botched Botox. Her hands are bruised too, dappled with purple, blue and green, and she has a sore wound like a crosshatch. The blood has dried from one cut until it is crusty and dark red.

'Oh my God,' Doris says. 'Oh, Lord.' She stares at Colleen, at the state of the house. 'Whatever's happened?'

Colleen is in such a rush to close the door that it catches Doris's arm. Her head and hands move at such a rate she is like a little nervous bird. She holds out her hand for Doris to help her back into a chair.

They sit still for a moment, Colleen hunched and tense despite the generous padding of the wingback. The house is normally immaculate. The party showed the place off perfectly, how house proud and tasteful Colleen is, and rightly so for it is an elegant, smart house, beautifully decorated, on a desirable street. But it has been vandalised and ransacked and whatever has been thrown on the floor by the burglars has stayed there. Colleen is too afraid to let Teddy out in the back garden so he has used the kitchen floor as his toilet.

'I should have come sooner … I should have come sooner,' Doris says.

Cleaning up Colleen's wounds and applying arnica gel to the bruises and disinfectant to the wound is a slow, agonising process. It is painful to watch because Colleen winces with every touch, Doris helps her upstairs and into bed as if Colleen were blind. Colleen smells of urine and sweat, but she wants to sleep now that someone is with her to help her feel safe. She can't remember the last time she slept; she's been too frightened to go upstairs to bed.

96

Doris leaves on a small sidelight and the landing light.

'Please, please, please … don't go.' Colleen's voice is barely audible.

Doris sees the two of them reflected in Colleen's dressing-table mirror, a beautiful cream-and-gold antique. She takes Colleen's hand and holds it gently. Lilac talc, a mascara and a glass perfume bottle are on the dressing table, like relics to vanity. A rose-velvet ottoman waits at the end of her bed.

'I'll stay, of course. I'll sleep next door.'

'I'm cold.' Colleen points to the bottom drawer in the mahogany wardrobe. 'In there.'

Doris fetches a soft blanket and then leaves strong, sweet tea and a packet of biscuits by Colleen's bedside, unsure when she may have last eaten. She has lost weight. So has Teddy.

'Check the windows and the front door, Doris.'

When Doris pulls the thick curtain aside to close the bedroom window, Colleen thinks she hears inhuman voices like animal cries in a jungle. She closes her eyes to the lurid shadows. 'You won't leave me, will you?' she asks.

'I promise.'

A horrible shadow follows Doris, not a fear of the burglars returning but a sadness for her friend who has vanished into herself, regressed to a child frightened of the dark, the boogie man, anything. Colleen's voice is feeble, a child's voice from the under the stairs, an afraid of thunder and lightning voice. The police haven't been informed. Should she call them?

Colleen shakes her head, wanting to be left alone, to never speak of the violence. Doris pulls the duvet up under her friend's chin and kisses her goodnight, growing more assertive with every second with the responsibility of having someone to protect.

In the morning Doris calls Andy before calling the doctor. She has to get to work but she doesn't want to leave Colleen on her own. Teddy is anxious about being left, so she takes him with her. Andy arrives within the hour, bombarding Doris with questions about Colleen which she answers as concisely as she can before running for the bus to work, pulling old Teddy along with her.

Colleen has a broken rib and bruising to her face and a deep cut to the hand. The physical injuries will heal but the real long-term damage isn't visible. At the end of the week, Mr Morris informs the staff at the Darwin that Colleen has decided to retire. The position of chief librarian will be advertised internally and externally in the near future. There is a sadness in the library that day, for Colleen has worked there for more than twenty years and is liked and respected by all.

Doris rushes home after work to pack a small overnight bag. The opened bottle of wine reminds her of her selfishness and self-indulgence. She pours the contents down the drain, its stench sickening her a little. It is an act she has done before. Many times.

Teddy is panting by the time they get to Colleen's house after a busy day. Colleen is still in bed but Andy says she has eaten something at least.

'I'll stay for as long as it takes, if you do what you can during the day,' Doris says assertively.

He nods and raises his eyebrows, seemingly surprised by her. She senses he wants to say something. The silence stretches out so she gets herself a glass of water. When her back is turned, he says, 'We've let her down. After everything's she done for us.' His voice cracks.

Doris reaches her arms around him as far as they will go. He sobs long deep sobs, his body jerking up and down. Doris fights back her tears, knowing he speaks the truth and they share the guilt.

'She's been through such a lot,' he says.

He tells Doris about Godfrey's terrible accident, the bed and the apparatus in her house long after he'd died, and the terrible burden of guilt Colleen had carried around needlessly, unbeknown to anyone. Doris listens in horror to Colleen's extraordinary life story – and yet Colleen has stayed so brave, generous in heart and dependable in every way to her friends, colleagues and neighbours.

Doris cries now at her own weakness and Colleen's strength and the giant heart inside Andy's chest, which she has foolishly and heartlessly bruised. The compassion and injustice she feels for Colleen after the attack and the burglary put her own situation into a new context.

'Come here,' Andy says and pulls her into a bear hug.

He prepares asparagus and new potatoes, salmon and dill. The butter melts slowly over the new potatoes on their way upstairs to Colleen as he carries her meal on a tray. Doris hides her surprise at his culinary skill by browsing Colleen's bookshelves. John never cooked once in their entire married life. The times when she was too unwell to cook or shop, he'd 'go hunting' which meant fish and chips, or Chinese takeaway if he was feeling flush. Andy explains that he has to thank his ex-wife for walking out on him and Jade when she was seven for developing competence and pleasure in the kitchen.

'I'm sorry.'

'It was a long time ago. Jade's twenty-four now. Time goes on.'

But it hasn't, not completely. Andy has got into a bad habit of sleeping in Jade's bed and calling her more than he should. He misses having her around, especially now she's in deep with Bosh and her Friday night visits have become shorter and shorter.

Doris washes the strawberries in the sink while Andy collects Colleen's tray. He is up there a long time. She starts eating the strawberries out of the colander, savouring the juicy freshness, the bright colour, the taste of summer. It seems there is a sense of the seasons with Andy in the food he prepares, which she hadn't thought about before. She shopped at Iceland when she cooked for John; now he has left, her staple diet is toast or sweet things.

Andy fills the sink with warm water and washing-up liquid before sitting down at the table to eat his strawberries. Doris shares out a packet of Minstrels to add a bit of chocolate to the mix. She likes the way Andy enjoys his food, how he hunches over it as if in prayer; it is a sacred intimate thing. He talks about the vegetables in season – the courgettes, squash, spring onions, runner beans – with a reverence that is hard not to admire. He tells her about his favourite summer dessert, Eton Mess. Doris's mouth waters at the description of meringue, cream and fresh berries. She has never tasted such a delicious combination.

Andy is starting his new job the next day, driving around the library bus. He says he is excited but a little nervous. 'I can drive right enough but I hope I don't get asked tricky stuff about books. Thrillers I'll be alright on.'

'Ring through to the library if you're not sure about something. They'll give you a mobile phone. Or use the search engine on the computer on the bus. I'll put together a list by genre that you could use. People like a chat when they choose a book, like they do when food is delivered. You've got all the experience you need.'

They are friends again by the time he and Louis leave for home. Doris feels something a bit more than that, which surprises her, but she knows she's blown her chances with Andy. He's forgiven her for standing him up and she can tell he is ready to fall for someone else. Someone very special.

Chapter Eighteen

14th September. A Friday. Lisa's birthday. Doris isn't sure if she is forty-three or forty-four, but she remembers the date. There's a calendar on most of the staff desks in the library – a rather old-fashioned idea in many ways.

John's birthday is at the beginning of December, too close to Christmas for anything really special. He liked to stay in, watch a movie, snuggle up on the sofa after steak and chips. It had been cosy, nice. Dull.

Doris focuses her attention on producing a list of books categorised by genre that will be available on the shelves in Babs, the library bus, for the next month. The categorisation is simple enough because the filter search does that for her, but the library readers' top-ten list takes more time. The computer lists users in the last ten weeks and their chosen books. She filters by age, gender and then reviews the list to look for trends.

Lisa Goodwood's names leaps from the page: *What to Expect when You're Expecting, Your Pregnancy Bible, The First Four Weeks with Your Baby.*

'Excuse me, do you have Imtiaz Dharker's latest book?'

The customer smiles at Doris as she closes one screen and opens another to search for the poet. Each of the customer's digits is clad in a silver ring, some with gems. Doris admires one thumb ring – a thick silver band edged with a strip of gold.

'The most recent book we have in stock at the moment is *Sari* published in 2004.'

The customer huffs and her shoulders deflate.

'Sorry,' Doris says. 'We don't have the space to stock everything, but I can request one from our Whitchurch branch.'

The young woman says she needs it today and saunters away, hitching her rucksack over one shoulder before pushing through the double doors. Doris pulls up her original screen. The return date on the book Lisa borrowed, *The First Four Weeks with Your Baby,* suggests she may have had her and John's child. Going on when the book was checked out, the baby will be somewhere around eight or ten weeks old. Two or three months. What is a baby like at that age? Smiling?

The book is overdue. Lisa's fine is mounting up each day. £2.06 and counting. Doris clicks on the address. It is out of date. She knows Lisa doesn't live there anymore.

***

At the end of the week, Andy prepares a special meal because he's finished his first full week in charge of Babs. Colleen is still taking her meals in bed with Teddy by her side, but she is gaining weight and starting to talk about routine things.

Doris can't wait for dessert – blackberry and apple pie, after baked aubergine and cheese. She hasn't sipped wine in almost a month, so when Andy pours her a small glass of red wine she hesitates.

'Do you prefer white? I got the red for the meal.'

'It's… I find it hard to have one. For the first time in a very long time, I've not touched a drop in nearly four weeks.' She stares at the tablecloth, ashamed of herself and her admission. 'I'm scared if I have one I'll—'

Andy laughs. 'Me too! I'm like that with fast food. Especially truck-stop food. Bacon sarnies, sausage sarnies. It's a drug, a habit. Yeah, I can easily gain a stone in a week if I let myself.'

'Really?'

Andy smiles at her. 'We're all human. Flawed. My daughter Jade is less than half my age and she's addicted to slimming products. If it's not eggs and oranges one week, it's Slim Fast, Weight Watchers, God knows what.'

'Colleen seems pretty straight and narrow.'

He nods a proud kind of nod, almost reverential. 'Yeah, she's a bit special.'

Doris tries to finish her meal. Lovely as it is, it won't all go down.

'I'm buying a house on Hollow Green, the new estate just off Barbados. I should get the keys soon.'

'Well, that's great.' He looks at her face. 'Isn't it?'

'Yes, it's— I have to pack up, you know. I've lived in what was the marital home for twelve years or more. It's going to be a fresh start. Properly alone. I mean, I stopped waiting months ago – but this is still

102

a big step.' Like seeing post addressed to Mr John Gambol and Miss Lisa Goodwood. Silly things confirm the finality of a catastrophic change.

His hand over hers is like Tupperware, it's so big and warm. The salt and pepper on the table are the only things in the way of their warm touch. He places another hand over hers. 'If I could have afforded to move to a new house after Catherine left me, I would have any day of the week. A place keeps its memories longer than you might want them. At times it feels haunted, like she hasn't left, except for—'

'The quiet.'

'Yes, and the sombre mood of the place. Catherine made it a home. Jade did her best but she was only young – seven when her mother left her. Later on Jade turned the house pink. For years her boyfriends have assumed I'm gay because of the décor. I don't care.' He shrugs. 'It's what I've got left of Jade under that roof.'

'I'm scared that I might – crumble. The move. It's— I'm not like Colleen.'

He pushes a piece of pie under her nose, the spoon already inserted into its middle. The sugar glistens, the pastry is baked to perfection. Inside the pastry, the fruit is fresh and hot and sweet. She only has to lift the spoon to her mouth.

'I'm sorry I missed my chance with you, Andy.'

He tilts his head to one side, exposing his thick neck, the smoothed skin part of him. It would be the place she'd kiss him but she knows he doesn't want her to. Instead, she tells him about the long weekend in Abersoch in a caravan with thin walls and three bedrooms, about the sea, the door closing on Christmas Eve and the funeral pyre in the back yard. She tells him about her miscarriage and her sorrow not to have experienced motherhood.

When she's finished, he clears away the bowls and washes up because life has to carry on. His broad shoulders at the sink and the smell of Fairy Liquid reassure her that keeping going is simply the best thing to do. The only thing.

The kitchen and downstairs toilet smell of bleach from their attempts to eradicate the signs of intrusion and disregard to this lovely home, so much so that Colleen can smell the bleach upstairs, which she likes. It is a smell of order, cleanliness.

Knowing how Colleen likes everything to have its place, they try to remember where the remaining ornaments and vases live in the lounge. After being ransacked, it still has an air of dishevelment despite Andy and Doris's efforts. It is a large room without Godfrey's bed. In its place, Andy and Colleen had put a small console table with a lamp and something else – Andy can't remember what. His knees click as he bends down to use a brush and pan to collect fragments of glass and hair.

Under Colleen's chair he finds a small piece of paper ripped from a notebook, which he automatically passes to Doris. She reads aloud:

It is my wish that I be left to die. My life as a person with paraplegia is not my own. My wife Colleen has agreed to honour my wish to let me die in bed at home. That is my final wish.

Godfrey

Neither of them knows what to say. Should he put the letter back and pretend not to have found it? He wants to. Doris looks horror-stricken. The room is very still and silent until Andy decides to put the letter in a drawer out of sight. They listen to him close it.

'It's not for us to know … or to judge.' He waits for a reply, a signal that Doris agrees to their pact to remain silent, ignorant about what may or may not have happened in that room.

Doris nods and creeps upstairs to bed. Andy and Louis have left by the time she gets to the top of the stairs. Her legs feel weary as she makes her way to her room. The light is still on in Colleen's bedroom; since the burglary, she has slept with a light on round the clock.

Doris gets ready for bed and then peeks her head around Colleen's door. Her friend is curved around Teddy, two perfect sleeping S shapes, too innocent and too mauled by life to be anything but victims at this moment in time.

Chapter Nineteen

Colleen hasn't been downstairs in her own home for over a month so Andy plans to force her downstairs to feed Teddy and to let him out for a much-needed wee. He and Doris have told her that they both have to work so she'll need to manage alone for a few hours. It pains Andy to see the distress on her brow and under her eyes when he explains what she needs to do, but he feels it is the best thing for her in the long run.

Since the burglary, Colleen has not asked for her Bible or for her friends to contact the local chaplain at Larkin Church. The gold crucifix she usually wears around her neck is in a drawer in her dressing table. It grieves her to think of the faded poppies on Godfrey's headstone – but not enough to rally the courage to leave the house.

All the locks have long been changed but still her routine is to ask her friends to check and check again that the windows and doors are locked. It has become a compulsion. Andy begins to worry she might never recover.

***

Doris would have preferred to take a driving lesson in natural sunlight but the instructor is fully booked on weekends and assures her that if she can cope with rush-hour traffic, she'll be ready to take her driving test in a matter of weeks.

So she does and she passes first time. Happy chemicals fizz through her head. The next day she buys Tina's yellow Beetle so Tina can get herself the new red Fiat she's been coveting. The Beetle doesn't have a sunflower on the dashboard but it does have a daisy. With a bit of work, Doris will soon eradicate the smell of cigarette smoke.

The first time she drives the Beetle, she winds down the window to feel the breeze run through her bobbed hair. She only drives to the doctor's surgery to pick up her prescription and then back home again, but she could go anywhere and that possibility is amazing. Mother is delighted for her and even goes as far as saying well done. She's probably expecting Doris to visit to take her out to the art shop for supplies.

A week before the deadline of 31st October, Doris receives papers from John's solicitors outlining the terms of their divorce. She has no desire to contest it and, having been naive enough to sign a prenuptial agreement before they got married, she signs and returns the paperwork the same day, together with her wedding ring.

The paperwork has come from a kind of non-universe, a vacuum of sorts, because she doesn't know where John and Lisa – or their child – are living. It makes them grow smaller, detached, in her eyes so that the signature on the dotted line means very little. It is an end to a half-nelson of a marriage.

If John had loved her, he wouldn't have succumbed to desire. Instead of seeing his adultery as an expression of her failing, she thinks of it as an expression of his unhappiness and disillusionment with their little marriage. It was a traditional marriage of routines but eleven years is a lot of marriage. She'd lost herself in that span and that, in many ways, is a crime worse than infidelity.

She and John are not so different, if the truth be known: they both have a biological need, his to sleep with Lisa, hers to have a child. She had loved him and, even now, if she lets herself she misses his warmth in bed beside her and his ridiculously loud laugh at the worst of jokes. The best times were in bed just before lights out, talking about their day, the things they'd seen, that had made them smile. Replayed and shared, they felt much brighter. The bedtime chats were the glue of the marriage and she misses them most.

It seems to her that, if it hadn't been Lisa, John would have slept with somebody else. It was just hard luck for her that it was her best friend. Just because he's committed adultery, it doesn't mean Doris is dull or useless. She can forgive herself. But them? The anniversary of his permanent exit through the front door flashes in the sky from time to time when she hears the click of high heels dying away or the finality of the latch closing on a door. The word 'sorry' still niggles at her, recurring before her eyes at times like moth wings.

John will be expecting her to creep meekly out of his house. She'd stopped cleaning the place as soon as her offer on 12 Hollow Green was accepted, particularly enjoying the build-up of dust mites on the blinds and window ledges, the grime of skin and hair in the bathroom. But that isn't enough. It is only a small tin of red paint but it has the deepest hue, peculiarly reminiscent of her miscarriage, so she sets to work in the bathroom – a splash at the bottom of the stairs and in the bedroom for good measure – red red red. Revenge isn't sweet. It's red.

The wardrobe gets worked over with her biker boot: first a single kick through each door and the back, then she rips out the drawers and stamps through them — cheap teak wood, lined with dust and stray hairs, a paperclip, a bead. She feels relieved; not a single photo, card, handwritten note or postcard flutter out to stab her in the ribs.

Next, she knifes the pillows from up high, watches the feathers shimmy down, some settling on the bed, some in the paint. What kind of man can't find at least a handful of words to explain why he is leaving his wife after eleven years? Doesn't he at least owe her that? She takes a black felt tip to write THANK YOU! on the grubby wallpaper in the lounge. He can take it how he likes.

She is tired of avoiding their regular haunts. If she bumps into him in an aisle in Tesco or a changing room in Fat Face then so be it. Posting the keys through the letterbox is just a perfunctory act, she tells herself. She has the things she is most sentimental about in her car – her books, those friends that saw her through the worst of what her husband did to her.

Later, she helps Andy pack up a few things at his house before he moves into Colleen's spare room. He is adamant that as soon as she has the key to 12 Hollow Green she must move in and sleep there. Part of her will miss their dinners, her chats with Colleen perched on the side of her bed, Teddy blowing bubbles or snoring. They've become a strange kind of family. It has pushed away the anxieties she had about leaving 42 Utkinton Street for good; instead, she will miss Colleen's chrome toast rack, the silver-handled knives in the magnetic knife block, and the meals that Andy prepares. She's learnt how to make delicious vegetable soup, chutney and has developed a taste for brie. She thinks she'll miss standing beside him at the kitchen sink, washing or drying depending on whose turn it is.

Will she miss the routines of home life with another person? The comfort and familiarity of it? Or miss Andy? The weeks at Colleen's have been like her own home before John left. The thought digs into her side like a stitch but she doesn't want to be trained to like marital routines – pillow talk, someone dictating that she watches *World's Strongest Man* and *Grand Slam of Darts* on TV. How can she undo the habits?

***

Each week Doris provides Andy with an updated list of books to help him answer queries relating to genre or popular choices. It means that she can't help but see what, if anything, Lisa Goodwood has chosen to read.

Andy doesn't need to use the list very often but it gives him confidence and pleasure to be able to answer queries when they occur. He is sad to leave Louis behind when he's at work; Louis had usually travelled with him on deliveries in his van but the library bus has limited space and some of its customers, often elderly, are frightened of dogs. But Louis and Teddy are becoming buddies and provide comfort to Colleen when she is home alone.

Doris starts experimenting with the library computer to see if it can make recommendations to readers based on their search history. With the odd exception, it can. The library team begins to spread the word about this new service and it soon takes off. It helps Andy streamline the books the bus accommodates and gives him a talking point with customers who sometime call in for a chat as well as a new book.

After a while, he asks Doris if he can enhance the choice of audiobooks on the bus instead of having such a lot of large print. Based on his experience and recommendations from staff, he doubles the choice and monitors how it is received. After a month, it's clear that audiobooks are popular and this section of the shelves expands further.

Andy talks about many of the audiobooks with infectious enjoyment. At one of his favourite spots, the car park of The Red Lion in Bamford, he likes to play an audiobook on low.

With Christmas just a few weeks away, they decorate the interior of the bus with tinsel. It worries him no end that Colleen still hasn't left the house.

'I know dogs aren't technically encouraged on Babs but Colleen might get on board with Teddy, offer the story dog service to children after school.'

Doris listens, hearing his concern. She reaches for a copy of Bab's timetable to see if there is a stop close to a school after three o'clock.

There is. Just one, but that's all they need. It makes sense to at least try it so, once Mr Morris has approved it, Andy gets to work cajoling Colleen out of the front door.

Chapter Twenty

Doris walks back from the corner shop on Saturday afternoon with a bag for life brimming with groceries for a meal she is going to cook for Tina that evening at Hollow Green. Her beret is pulled at an angle against the breeze, and a women's magazine she's bought on a whim protrudes shamelessly from her bag. A sherbet lemon works its way in the inside of her mouth, sticking to her teeth on the right side, making it difficult to say 'hello' to someone on the estate without spitting a bit out.

She especially loves her pristine white bathroom and the jade-green tiles in the shower cubicle, so her shopping bag contains bath salts and a scented candle.

The curtains at next door's window are fashionably yellow and grey. A discreet blind hangs at the kitchen window. They park their car next to hers, half on the kerb, as the two-bedroom houses don't have a parking spot, but her mysterious neighbour works longer hours than she does. From the upstairs window, she's eyed the table and chairs in the back garden in readiness for dry, warm weather. Her garden is still a blank postcard, getting ready for a few words when the weather warms up. She has plans to remove some turf to create a border. Something colourful. Not red.

Two boys whizz by on bikes, clouds of breath streaming from their mouths; on a mission, perhaps, an adventure to the far end of the estate and back. Less than a mile, but still. The one with a blue hood makes a tractor sound when he turns his bike around.

Doris fumbles the key into the lock and steps inside to the smell of the new carpet. Calm washes over her.

The glossy magazine is full of insights; she feels glad she is only just learning about some of the topics. Recipes, diets, celebrity break-ups; the inane chatter flickers across her eyes. It offers top tips on how to spot if your husband is having an affair. Doris's blissful ignorance protected her from expending energy on sniffing shirts, detecting more bathing or a new cologne, or new underpants, or…

She puts the magazine down and sighs, luxuriating in the peace and the sponginess of her new sofa and the benefits of naivety. Irritatingly, something else the magazine said has caught her attention: most affairs last just three to six months. Are John and Lisa still together? She retrieves the magazine and reads the rest of the article, wishing she could read it under tarpaulin by torchlight.

For a figure like Doris's, November is a great month for clothes and feet. Swathed in the colours of autumn, her skinny legs wrapped in biker boots over dark leggings or woolly tights, her jumper dresses and cord pinafores – all the things she loves to wear all year round – become fashionable once the clocks go back.

Doris spends more time than ever looking at herself in her mirror under the lights in the immaculate bathroom, turning her face at different angles to decide which is her best side. After flossing and hair brushing, she has a new habit of reading on the toilet. Living alone in a home of her own choice has its nuances. They are still dating one another.

Tina arrives later that evening to wolf Doris's spaghetti Bolognese and update her on the movements on Utkinton Street. Doris doesn't pretend to hide her interest; Tina's her mate, she knows a lot of what there is to know.

'I'm convinced John has moved in – your John, but different. He used to have quite a lot of hair, didn't he?'

Doris nods. 'Who else? I mean, is Lisa in there with his baldness?'

'That's the thing. It's not Lisa. I've seen the same woman go in and leave about a half-hour later, but she's a lot younger than Lisa – like blonde, spiky-hair kind of age.'

Doris doesn't know what to make of this surveillance. 'You sure it's John?'

'Yeah, his van's there. It's him. Honest to God. And you know what's weird. He's lost all his hair and there's a bed in the lounge.'

Some floor in Doris's stomach drops, like a lift in reverse, a sudden descent down the cliff face of her intestines. She feels something is very wrong in Tina's finger painting.

Doris excuses herself to the downstairs loo to take a few deep breaths in private. The miniature basin can only accommodate vomit from Lilliputians, so she hovers over the toilet seat just in case.

Nothing spews, just a bit of excessive spit. She suddenly craves a glass of wine but has nothing in stock.

Tina doesn't know about the desiccated furniture, the pillows she plucked or the paint she generously poured. That is between her and John and whoever else is in that house with him.

Doris asks Alexa to play 'White Ladder' by David Grey. It's one of their favourites; it puts her in a better mood.

'What's your next-door neighbour like?' Tina asks, with a breadstick protruding from her nicotine-stained teeth, a surrogate cigarette, oblivious to Doris's ashen complexion.

'I can't say, except they work longer hours than me and do a good job of keeping themselves to themselves. Maybe I need to get a bad cough?'

Tina smiles. 'Maybe you do. Or you could go around to introduce yourself.'

After dinner and goodbyes, Doris counts to thirty before getting in her car. Tina is a speedy driver, so she figures she'll be almost home by the time she, Doris, sets off. An orange glow from the streetlights and the standard outside light fitted to each dwelling allays her fears as she climbs into her car and speeds away. The darkness of the sky and the quietness of the roads turn her thoughts to Colleen and Andy, to the gentle progress she is making to trust the world again.

Doris drives by her old house once, inches away from John's parked van and Tina's rosy Fiat, and then turns the conspicuous yellow Beetle around to park at the far end of Utkinton Street.

Once the wheels stop moving and the engine dies, she asks herself what on earth she is doing here. With her head on the over-sized steering wheel, she closes her eyes and tries to find clarity in the chaos of thought. She bangs the steering wheel, frustrated with her inability to let go, move on, switch off and all those other clichés she hates that describe her state perfectly.

The slam of the car door is loud and long in the night sky, forcing her to hurry her pace away from the offending car in the direction of number 42. A few feet away from John's house, she gathers that the lounge curtains are open and a sight will be revealed, a sight she anticipates to be as intimate as the one between her legs.

She edges past, one foot in front of the other; her face turns, her heart beats loud, too loud, but still something inside her makes her look, look, look. She wishes the curtains were shut, like legs closed, the secret cave, the opening blocked, but they're not; the view is exposed, rare, bright in the artificial light.

Doris sees inside and immediately veers in front of a passing car to cross the road to get away from the room. She runs back to her parked car, throws herself into the driver's seat, starts driving even before the seat belt is on so she can move into the darkness, away from the street lights, so the darkness can wrap itself around her skull, her wide unblinking eyes. She drives on automatic pilot and robotically enters her new home, where she weeps and she weeps for the man that used to look like John.

They make her drink. Guzzle until her stomach is a well, so full it begins to pour over the top and trickle down Utkinton Street, a red rivulet, an S shape all the way to the corner shop and back. They still make her drink, sip it if she has to, faces at the bottom of the glass. She keeps drinking, swaying, and they are still watching. Then it is dark, the colour of a drinker's liver.

Chapter Twenty-One

Doris loves her job but Monday is a long day; not just a shock after the weekend off, but a late-night opening until seven o'clock. The paracetamol keep the hangover at bay as she works on producing an updated list of recommendations and new releases in stock for Andy.

As always, the name Lisa Goodwood shouts at her from the printout. The address is still out of date, which annoys Doris because she likes to be efficient. There is no mobile number, just an email address. Before she considers her actions, she fires off a standard email asking for an updated address and a contact number. There is no fine outstanding, so at some point Lisa has returned the baby books to a library but it isn't possible to trace which one. She could have dropped them off at any of the libraries in Shropshire, of which there are several.

Doris is happy to let the library staff and volunteers choose their hours over the Christmas and New Year period. She is the only single person without children, except for Andy, who has more or less confirmed his relationship with Colleen. The last time she visited Colleen, she sensed his permanence at her place, a belonging as he put one hand on the polished banister to say goodbye at the front door.

In the library they've used the traditional themes of the time of year to promote new and old releases: Harvest, Halloween, Bonfire Night, Christmas. The Man Booker Prize list causes a surge of interest in literary fiction and then the children's reading activities start over the Christmas period.

Colleen refuses to leave her home despite the demand for the story dog, but she has ventured downstairs and stuck a slippered toe into her back garden. After almost a year in her job, there is less and less that is unknown and daunting to Doris. Keeping up the high standards Colleen set is a motivation each day, as are the eclectic customers that grace the Darwin, from the weird to the wonderful. The library has a heart and a soul that it offers to the many people who come to life inside its walls.

Doris struggles to concentrate on her work once four o'clock comes round. Her thoughts return to 42 Utkinton Street, to her ex-husband. The term doesn't change anything; their lives are still enmeshed in her memory, the synapses haven't separated him from her psyche like the divorce papers suggest they should. Why hasn't he got any hair? And who's the woman Tina mentioned? And where is Lisa? If only he'd spoken to her before walking out on her to explain his actions, his ill-health.

'Can I join the library?'

Doris is jolted from her reverie by a polite request from a well-dressed man carrying a large leather satchel. She notices his long elegant fingers as she enters his details on the computer. She releases an oooh sound when she enters Mr Russell Bromley's address.

'I'm Doris. I live next door to you.'

He looks puzzled for a second. 'I wasn't sure anyone was living there.' He offers his hand to shake.

'I haven't got around to putting up curtains yet,' she says by way of explanation, as the house is somewhat embryonic. They chat about the design and the convenient location to the town centre.

'It's a pleasant development, I must say. Just wish I had skylight! It has everything else on my list.'

Doris smiles at the idea. She, too, had once wanted a skylight.

She knows she is going to open a bottle of wine before she gets the key in the lock. The hollow feeling is there, the place where the avocado stone should be. In the sweet spot between being tipsy and inebriation, she calls her mother.

'About time! I was beginning to think you'd died! I'm eighty next week, in case you've forgotten.'

'You could have phoned me, Mother.'

'Couldn't! I don't have your new number. I know you've moved because your old number's out of use. Glad my money came in useful, Doris,' she says bitterly.

Doris recalls one bright spring afternoon when she was around sixteen, sitting at the Formica-topped kitchen table eating her supper. Her mother was ironing. She remembers the cable snaking from the socket to the ironing board, steam hissing at intervals as her mother struggled to flatten a very creased blouse, the flesh jangling under her arms.

Doris doesn't hear the gentleness in her mother's voice as she says goodbye. All she notices is the fact that she has to repeat her new phone number four times before her mother writes it down correctly.

'Have you got that, Mother?' she asks sharply. She listens intently. 'You're not crying, are you?'

'Just a sniffle. It's that time of year.'

It is so difficult to communicate. It has been like that for as long as Doris can remember. After the phone call, dull pain in her temples takes her upstairs to the bathroom for a soak.

A queer thought pops into Doris's brain as she lies in the bath, the water a milky hue from the bath salts and soap she's used. She is snug and forgetful in her new bathroom, luxuriating in fantasy. Perhaps Mr Russell Bromley is in his bath on the other side of the wall? The layout of his house is the same as hers.

The sound of a car engine and headlights interrupt her thoughts. That's probably him now, late again from wherever it is he works. Thoughts of the summer come to her – a readiness to hear lawnmowers, strimmers, smell the smoke from barbecues when evenings are elastic, stretching the light out across the sky for longer. From the opened window she hears a mother call, 'James. James. It's time to come in. Bedtime.'

She has a large cardboard box to unpack, items from Andy's house that Jade and Bosh don't want now they've moved in together. Andy's warned her that they are an acquired taste, mostly pink and girlie, a kind of fairy-tale décor. He offered them soon after he and Colleen visited her and expressed surprise at her minimalist taste. Doris concedes that her house is very beige and sterile, the very opposite of the last lived-in home.

Over coffee, Colleen had joked about not needing post-it notes anymore because she has Andy to watch over her. Doris had felt a little jealous, but only for a second. Colleen has regained some of her briskness, the headteacher sort of presence that smacks of being practical and capable. It is a relief to see her dressed and out of her house.

A heart-shaped candy dish decorated with tiny shells prompts Doris to lift it to her ear to listen for the rush of the sea. The single painting is a watercolour of a female nude, no face just the narrow rope of her spine and the knot of her chignon at the base of her neck. Her cello curves beg to be stroked and yet she is standing alone in a room, facing away from the painter. Doris thinks it an odd kind of composition. What of her face, her expression? Or is the mystery of her the essence of the painting? If she saw her face, stroked her curves, the model would be known, surrendered. Is that the point?

Doris carries the painting to the lounge where she wedges it behind a bookend on a bookshelf and makes a mental note to purchase a hammer and nails.

The piggy bank comes out of the box last. An understated pink with a generous slot for coins. It has a purpose. Doris drops in a few pennies just to hear the sound in its skeleton. It is a litany of hers. A coin for John to be well; a coin for Colleen and Andy to live out their days happily together forever; a coin for Jade and Bosh to get married; a coin for Mother to be well and pleasant.

In bed, the same queer thought comes to her. Mr Russell Bromley is perhaps on the other side of the wall, horizontal, an offering to the night on a slab of cool cotton. She could make herself fall in love with the idea of him if she chooses to. He could be the hero in the short story she might write one day, wearing the aftershave of her choice; he could be the addressee on a postcard from a holiday she might take. So many possibilities. Perhaps he plays the flute with those beautiful hands? Perhaps he practises scales from morn till night.

She vows not to get to know Mr Russell Bromley; she prefers her version of him and the ignorance of not knowing his preferred biscuits, his morning routine, his relationship with his mother, how he likes his eggs. The man on the opposite side of the wall will remain perfect with perfectly elegant hands – a perfect stranger.

Chapter Twenty-Two

Colleen walks into Larkin church a full half an hour before the service is due to start so she can sit discreetly towards the back on a side aisle. There is a thin man with a disagreeable expression handing out hymn books, a face she doesn't recognise. A couple sitting two pews ahead make murmured remarks then look round, ostensibly at the architecture and the stained-glass window at the rear of the church.

There is a surge of people five minutes before the service is due to start, which quickens Colleen's heartbeat, so she ducks down on the kneeler and prays. She is wearing her crucifix around her neck. As she prays, she catches the smell of incense and the familiar tones of Father Theo. She was once a regular worshipper and she'd liked the amiable, plumpish priest.

As she returns to sitting on her pew, the only person on it, Father Theo nods his head at her having recognised her face. The subtlety of the gesture means a lot, dissipating some of the unease she feels. The reassuring pattern of the service and the familiar places when the congregation say 'Amen' help Colleen to reunite with God.

After the service, she warmly shakes Father's hand and makes to leave before a conversation can commence. She hurries through the churchyard, past the yew, not even pausing at Godfrey's grave. A crow takes flight as she walks briskly through the lych gate, noticing the snowdrops in the graveyard grass and the mellow light. The church and the mellifluous rhythm of the service still make sense to her but she has no desire to spend time in the graveyard with the moss-covered headstones while she still has the life in her to walk away.

She is in love with Andy, and he with her. Life has moved on in the best kind of way.

***

Dr Timpson says she should update her list of what she's good at now that she's passed a driving test and bought a car. He says that's two good things but she thinks it is really only one, so she puts them on the same line in her blue-and-white spotty notebook.

118

Since she got the car, her levels of exercise have dropped so she questions whether she can still have 'takes regular exercise' on her list. But he's told her not to be so hard on herself. Their conversations are invaluable but occasionally she feels like a little bird flying into a window pane of glass.

'What makes you smile, Doris?' he asks, while leaning forward in that consultative doctor way that he has. She doesn't know, so when she gets home she starts a separate page for that which, with hindsight, has several items crossed out:

~~Opening a bottle of wine~~
~~Sleeping all day~~
~~Daydreaming about revenge~~
On a fresh page she begins again:
Tina
Andy
Colleen
Eating chocolate in bed
Looking at the moon
Robins
Driving my yellow car
Book club discussions
Mother's gifts (knickers as well as money)
My yellow scarf
My bathroom
Darwin library
Puck
Doris is surprised by the length of her list: happy chemicals fizz.

The following week, Dr Timpson explains that it's not events themselves that can cause mental ill-health, it's the way we interpret them. And sometimes, when we aren't well, we interpret things differently to others.

***

Andy likes people-watching in the library, typically while sitting on the ground floor in a soft chair between fiction and large print. It's an area that has a section on health and four computers for customers to use. The audiobook section is upstairs but he's picked up a random book to look the part.

Snatches of conversation amuse him:

Vicky's put on some weight
No loo rolls
Brilliant ending
Warm coat
Renewal

He doesn't know how to tell Colleen he can't read very well – she'll think he's stupid – but he doesn't want to keep secrets from her. He gets by, but that's all. She deserves the very best of him, the best version he can be. He can only pretend not to read her handwriting or forget his glasses for so long. Jade's always helped him or showed him how to use technology to get by; that is embarrassing enough, but Colleen is intelligent and well-read… He hides his chin in his duffle-coat.

He loves to listen to someone reading. His favourite voice is Jeremy Irons, who narrates *Angel Hearts* and *Brideshead Revisited*. On Tuesdays, Colleen reads to the under-fives' group and that's a treat too. She has a knack of adopting different voices for each character. The teenagers in the library seem very smart to Andy, reading books of three hundred pages or more on their phones, or the students from Europe reading a novel in English – it blows him away.

Colleen says Doris is working on a collection of short stories and secretly longs to be published. That would be something, to listen to a book written by a friend. Mr Morris is delighted Colleen has rescinded her resignation.

He's so proud of Jade and happy she likes Colleen. He was nervous about telling her, but she was happy for him and said, 'About time, Dad.'

Is it in stock?
Phone charger

Sleeping in a double bed beside Colleen feels strangely natural but, given that there's two of them, it's only like each of them having a single bed; they happen to be joined up and under a shared duvet. Colleen is neat, even in sleep: her arms stay by her sides all night long. He likes to look at her when she's asleep, the only time the separate parts of her face stop moving, and her breath is even and soothing to listen to.

A regular customer mutters something indecipherable to himself. The middle-aged man with a wide girth always comes alone, carrying a yellow furry rucksack in the shape of a giant yellow M&M on his front and a similar red rucksack on his back, like a suicide bomber of sweets. The giant Ms and the bright colours single him out from the flow of the room. The rucksacks might be something he's collected coupons for. They look like a practical solution to staying warm or carrying around library books as he browses the large print section for some time before taking his mutterings into the lift. The room is bland for a moment until someone else comes along.

Andy catches a glimpse of Colleen on her way back to the central desk. He admires her upright posture and the accessories she wears, which are always colour coordinated. He pulls in his stomach. She's the one for him; he knows that already. He'd been longing to devote himself to be a beautiful person and the ironic thing was that she was there all the time. It took a vicious burglary to find out.

She can't apply mascara or paint her nails because she says her hand still shakes a bit. He'd like to go over to tell her she looks beautiful but she'd be embarrassed. He'll tell her later when he cooks her dinner: prawn risotto.

He and Doris never mention the letter from Godfrey. From time to time he thinks about it but he stands true to what he said to Doris: they don't know what it was like, and they are not in any position to judge. It was a kindness, a big kindness, that took its toll on Colleen. He knows that better than anyone, having removed that redundant bed from the lounge long after it should have been out of sight.

Chapter Twenty-Three

It takes Doris longer than usual to dress on Sunday morning, not because she's got up earlier than normal for a weekend but because she's driving to Carlisle to see Mother. The car had a birthday clean after work on Saturday, inside and out. For some strange reason, she also emptied the contents of her handbag to dispose of old receipts, sweet wrappers, cookie crumbs, rubbish that is normally quite happy to stay in there until the bag comes to the end of its life.

Mother had sounded sceptical when Doris said she'd be visiting but wouldn't be staying long because she had the journey home and work the next day. Mother asked why she hadn't booked the Monday off so she could stay over and Doris couldn't find a good reason.

Dr Timpson says to listen to music from time to time to boost her mood so she listens to the radio, switching between Smooth and Radio Two until the signal for Smooth isn't soothing her at all. By then the landscape is more familiar, releasing a surprising sense of calm.

When she is about twenty minutes away from Mother's house, Doris pulls into a service station. It's not that she desperately needs a pit-stop but she does want to gather herself before arriving. In the toilet cubicle, she takes deep breaths to steady her racing heart. She tries to push through the feelings of anxiety and stress to expose the thought that is doing this to her – the painting of her. Her mother painted her as defeated and weak and it is too much to bear. Doris can't bear the look of pity in her mother's strokes or her eyes.

Nerves bring on a nasty bout of diarrhoea. Doris is glad to be anonymous as she comes out of the cubicle to leave the toxic stench behind for the next poor soul. At least the toilet seat is warm – every cloud...

Mother opens the door looking like she's just walked out of a salon. Her hair is curled like fat sausage rolls and she is coated in a floral scent. Her eyesight isn't what it was but she's applied a spot of rouge on each cheek as expertly as she can. She looks like a doll.

She puts one hand on Doris's shoulder and looks genuinely surprised to see her. Before she can embrace her, Doris steps back and says, 'You've shrunk!' Hanging in the hall is a painting of a cherub. 'Did you paint that?'

'Yes, do you like it?' Irene touches the framed glass as gently as if it were a baby's face; her arthritic fingers are bent where they shouldn't be.

'I do. You've improved.'

Irene beams and ushers Doris into the lounge, where she has positioned a cake stand with two cupcakes and a butterfly cake on a coffee table.

'Did you make those?' Doris asks.

'No, a friend did. I'll make the tea,' Irene says, and bustles into the kitchen like there is a queue.

They have the best conversation while Irene is in the kitchen, shouting to Doris. They talk about the weather, the journey, all the usual things, but there is an atmosphere of excitement, joy even, that loses its way when they come face to face. They prefer to avoid eye contact because neither of them wants to see pity in the other's eyes.

Doris thinks Mother looks shorter and thinner. The house is unchanged apart from her own wedding photograph, which has tactfully been removed at some stage. There's a pile of novels by her mother's chair, which must be there for Doris's benefit as Irene has never read fiction and ridiculed Doris's interest in it as a waste of time.

What Doris knows is that she has a history here.

'I've got your bedroom ready, just in case,' Irene says, sounding a little plaintive, but Doris doesn't notice. She's too busy not looking at the oil painting of herself.

'I can't stop, Mother. I told you that.'

'Another time, then.'

Irene carries a tray of tea into the room. At any moment Doris expects it to go crashing to the floor but it makes it down onto the table.

'I'll pour,' Doris states because her nerves might not take much more. 'You look well. I like your pearls.'

Irene fingers them, over and over. 'They were my mother's. They'll be yours one day.'

For as long as Doris can remember, Mother has had a habit of sitting with her legs wide open. It was a deterrent to bringing

123

boyfriends or friends home during that stage when a blush was never far away.

Doris gives her a box of sugar-free chocolates. They probably taste disgusting but at least Irene can't grumble about her cholesterol.

'Did you put sugar in?'

'I can't remember.'

Doris heads to the pantry. It is a time warp, the best kind; she loves the pantry, always has, and it hasn't changed at all. The shelves are still lined with jars and crockery and the hooks on the back of the door give a home to T-towels and a bag stuffed with foil and cling film. The plastic mould in the shape of a rabbit is there, well used years ago for blancmange or jelly. There are the old biscuit tins Irene uses to keep cake fresh.

Eventually, Doris finds the sugar in a stripy porcelain jar labelled *Sugar*. Obviously. Doris makes a mental note to add Mother's pantry to her list of things that make her smile.

'We should have lunch!' Irene suddenly announces. The clock on the mantelpiece says it's twelve-thirty.

'We've only just had cake.'

Irene either doesn't hear Doris or chooses to ignore her as she bustles into the kitchen. Doris can hear plates and cutlery clinking. The sounds take her back in time to sitting on this very seat, just back from school, hungry and cross that Mother's efforts to make her a nice tea take too long. Patience was never one of Doris's virtues. After being a wife, she thinks back to those prepared meals with gratitude.

'Ready!'

It's a familiar chime. Doris skips into the kitchen, happy to be a daughter again, her mother fussing over her with all her favourite foods, including steamed chocolate pudding and custard. Not home made like they used to be, but still delicious. Perhaps Irene does love her a little bit.

Doris appraises the mother in her life, framed by the kitchen sink, the soap suds on the coffee cup, the glass. She sees her now as tough, independent, caring. If only Irene believed in her, thought she was gifted. If only they shared interests.

After she's eaten the equivalent of her body weight, she offers to take Mother shopping for a new bra as she isn't wearing one.

124

'I'm a feminist. I don't need a bra.' Irene chuckles and points to a copy of *Women and Power* by Mary Beard, which sits side by side with the washing-up brush on the window ledge.

They talk about a birthday party Doris had in the house when she was about eleven. It was a kind of disco, with music and a few boys. Mother wanted to help Doris make a few friends, settle into secondary school, and the party had helped. Happy chemicals make the time with Mother pass quickly; there is not a single criticism or put down to spoil the entire afternoon.

Chapter Twenty-Four

Andy's original plan was to book a table at a new seafood restaurant in Shrewsbury, which Colleen's friends have raved about, but then Jade comes up with a better idea: a home-cooked meal, served by her, at his old house now that it is occupied by Jade and Bosh.

At first he thinks it sounds a bit ordinary and corny but on reflection he realises that Colleen will be more comfortable in familiar surroundings. And, as Jade has pointed out, the décor is perfect for a romantic meal for two.

Together with the food shopping, he purchases four new candle bulbs for the chandelier in the lounge. He'd removed the bulbs years ago, tired of breaking them each time he knocked his head against them. Jade helps him set up the table immediately under the chandelier. With the fairy lights switched on, with all the pink and the chintz, it is a perfect cliché enhanced by the single red rose on the table and a heart-shaped balloon that Jade produces at the last minute and ties to the back of Colleen's chair.

Jade, dressed in black with a white apron that she's borrowed from a friend, is there to greet Colleen with a glass of wine and take her smart woollen coat when she arrives. Wearing makeup, the only physical scar from the burglary and assault that Andy and Jade can see is a cut to her hand. They take in the fact that she is wearing red shoes; it is a sign that Colleen is feeling good about the evening. Andy is clean-shaven and wearing a freshly ironed checked shirt.

As she tops up their wine glasses, Jade noticed that the reserve in her dad's eyes disappears when he talks to Colleen.

Colleen doesn't put her hand to her mouth when she laughs as much. The guilt of enjoying life has gone.

'Alexa, play "What a Wonderful World" by Louis Armstrong.'

Colleen smiles as the song plays. Doris has lent Andy her Alexa so they can choose the right song for the moment.

Colleen was very upset that one of her favourite ornaments was broken during the burglary; it was a glass ornament of a little girl holding a balloon. But, with help from Jade, Andy's found a replica on the internet which arrived just in time for him to wrap it and give it to her over dinner.

He has chosen a menu that reflects his personality and food loves. They start with thick, wholesome, home-made soup with a warm roll and soft butter, followed by beef with red wine, the finest oyster mushrooms and chopped parsley with sticky honey and Madeira sauce. For dessert, they have chocolate gateau with the sweetest, brightest, cherry coulis – it needs a glasshouse, not a dessert cabinet. To finish, grapefruit-sharp sorbet.

If Colleen decides to stay over, which he hasn't assumed for one moment that she will, he is ready to supply pastry in the morning – *pain au chocolat* and freshly squeezed orange juice, or smoked salmon and scrambled eggs with cracked pepper and piping-hot coffee if she prefers.

'Alexa, play "Dreamlover" by Sam Cooke.'

He's had to respect Colleen's wish not to go to the police to report the theft of her handbag from the library and then the burglary and assault at her house, so they avoid the subject. He wonders whether her reluctance to go to the police comes from a sense of guilt about committing a crime by granting Godfrey's wish – but he isn't sure if she did grant the wish or not. He doesn't know; most likely he never will but that's alright because he knows she is a beautiful, good person. She says that with every kindness, every morsel of food and sip of wine, the footprints of the intruders are erased. They are not indelible; that is something.

'I'd love to drive Route 66 one day, the Mother Road,' Andy confesses over dessert.

'In a Mustang!' Colleen suggests with more enthusiasm than he was anticipating.

'No, a Winnebago. Customised, of course. There's never enough cup holders, I find.'

They talk about the food the route might afford them over and above the fast food from pit stops. Andy divulges that Jade has never grown out of her fondness for chicken nuggets, chips and baked beans, a staple meal in front of the television after school.

'What food are you?' Colleen asks, smiling a little flirtatiously.

Andy's bottom lip sticks out while he thinks. 'I'd like to think I'm a rock cake – or broth, perhaps. I'd say Jade is a chocolate coffee-cream fancy or a passion-fruit crème. You're a honeyed parsnip. A papaya. Doris – Neapolitan ice cream!'

'I did think about becoming vegetarian when Godfrey and I were holidaying in Greece, but we lived on seafood – the swordfish and lemon, and the paella with the juiciest, fattest prawns and the tenderest of rice were amazing. But here, especially when it's cold and raining, I just want a Sunday roast or a steak.'

'Perhaps I should go veggie. I need to lose a few pounds.'

'Don't be daft. The only thing you need is a dishwasher!'

They talk about visiting the markets in Barcelona in the spring and indulging their romance with food by cooking things for each other they've never contemplated before.

After Colleen swallows the last fork full of gateau, she lets out a contented sigh. 'That was superb! It's fair to say I have well and truly got my appetite back! It's funny how food always tastes better when someone else cooks. Just walking into your house and being greeted by the wonderful smells of cooking – it's quite an aphrodisiac!' She laughs behind her hand.

'What food would you say I am?' he asks shyly.

She reaches for his hand across the table. 'You're the seasoning every meal needs.'

'Alexa, play "Unchained Melody" by Sam Cooke.'

He laughs from his belly and she notices that his tongue is stained with claret. The starched white napkins fall to the floor as he takes her hand and leads her upstairs to bed for the icing on the cake.

Chapter Twenty-Five

Mother's semi is a time machine. Sleeping in her old bedroom transports Doris back to her teenage self when she was obsessed with Stephen King's horror stories and writing short stories of her own. She sees some of her old favourites are still there on the bookshelf looking well-thumbed and dog-eared, as good books should. The single bed is neatly made up with a patchwork quilt and a generous stash of blankets because the radiator has never worked properly. The white dressing table is still under the window but the paraphernalia of teenage beauty is long gone. It has recently been dusted because she can see where Mother has missed a bit. Irene needs to have a cataract removed in her right eye so she can see properly.

Doris takes a look at herself in the mirror and sees her mousey hair and eyes and generous lips; they are neither attractive nor unpleasant. But what bothers her is that there is no trace of happy chemicals in the defeated gaze in her eyes or the exhausted position of her shoulders. Defeated. That's the word. Her mother has more chutzpah and get up and go in her face – and that's not been airbrushed, because Doris has spent the last few hours looking at it. The likeness between them strikes her.

'I don't want to be like this anymore.'

During their last appointment, Dr Timpson said people can choose what defines them if they work hard on controlling their thoughts and feelings. He gently asked her whether she wanted to be defined by her ex-husband, ex-friend, miscarriage. No. No. No. What then? He didn't say that but she did, to herself, when she drove home.

She sleeps through the whole night; waking up is a revelation after nine hours of uninterrupted sleep. Her mother's snores carry across the landing. In the bathroom, Mother's teeth grin at her from the side of the basin. The pink pot containing the gnashers needs a wash so Doris braves it and removes the grunge with her finger. It seems unkind to use Mother's beige face flannel.

Doris must love her deep down. If she let herself, she could love her a lot.

She doesn't notice the pearls scattered about.

Mother kept a vegetable patch when Doris was at secondary school; she grew cabbages, onions, carrots and potatoes. The garden has been dug up since and showered with gravel. It irks Mother that she can't have a lawn or grow a few flowers but she can't mow or dig anymore, and paying someone is out of the question. She has a single pot in the back garden that she can see from both the window at the sink and the lounge window. It's a terracotta pot with a fuchsia in it. Beautiful. A butterfly has already shown its appreciation.

Doris loses track of time as she enjoys breakfast – marmalade on toast, which she never eats at home. After a third slice, she wonders why. She's been enjoying watching great tits at the bird feeders and then tidying up downstairs. Most of the pictures on the wall are wonky but she decides she likes them like that and leaves them alone.

She remembers a time when she dressed her mother's artificial Christmas tree in pink-and-blue clothes pegs and paper clips. Instead of crackers, she made bookmarks with quotations from *Twelfth Night* written in her very best handwriting. She used a new pen, a glittery one, which made it especially hard to be neat. Mother loved singing, especially carols with high notes and an upbeat rhythm. Her favourite was 'Good King Wenceslas', which Doris struggled to say when she was little much to the amusement of Mother and her friends. Every year a snow globe came from some safe place, a rare ornament in their house, placed on the bureau with the photo frames.

When she sees it's eleven o'clock, she races up the stairs into Mother's bedroom. It is still dim with the curtains drawn but too quiet for comfort. Doris's heart is racing with fear that her mother has died in her sleep. She leans over the mound in the bed under a hundred covers and reaches for her mother's arm. The mound suddenly moves.

'What on earth are you doing, Doris? You gave me such a fright!'

'You and me both. It's eleven o'clock.'

'So?'

'What time do you usually get up, Mother?'

The ping-pong goes back and forth until Doris grows so exasperated that she draws the curtains to release a wonderful beam of sunlight across the stacked eiderdowns and their swirls of gold, green and orange.

'Mother! What's happened to your face?' Doris rushes over to the bed. 'And your hand is all cut.'

'Stop fussing. I fell on the way to the bloody bathroom, that's all. Don't fuss. My pearls are—'

'Fuss! I'm calling the doctor. Why didn't you get me up?'

'I didn't want to bother you. My knees hurt,' Mother says, pulling the covers back.

Her knees are grazed from the fall and from crawling back to bed. Doris feels tearful and blinks a lot as she applies the Savlon. Then she crawls on her hands and knees across the landing to retrieve the fallen pearls from the broken necklace because Irene wants them.

'How many have you got?'

'More than ten.' The doorbell goes. 'Who will that be?'

'Beats me.'

Doris places the pearls in Mother's outstretched hand. She runs down the stairs in a flap. 'Can I help you?'

'You must be Doris!' The woman dressed in bright colours waves a lanyard and smiles broadly. 'I'm Natalie, from the Carlisle Wildlife Trust. Feed the Birds. I come every week to top up the bird feeders, chat to your mum.'

'Come in. She's still in bed.'

'Is Irene alright?' Natalie walks straight into the lounge where she usually sits with Irene. It would be impolite to ask her to leave. She takes the chair beside Mother's and Doris gets a sense of routine. Even Natalie's shoes are jolly colours: swirling purple and red with a buckle. Her greying hair is cut short, but she looks feminine with her jangly green earrings and sparkly eye-shadow. She's a bit older than Doris and wearing well, by the looks of it.

'Had a fall in the middle of the night. Bruising mainly, I think, but the doctor's going to call in later.' Doris tries to relax her shoulders by leaning against the seat of the sofa, but it feels awkward so she sits upright with her hands in her lap. She notices Natalie's wedding ring.

'Poor thing. Irene hates being in bed. Last time, she twisted her ankle.'

'She never said.'

Natalie explains enthusiastically that Feed the Birds is a befriending scheme. Her eyes crinkle when she smiles. She is trained to be an extra pair of eyes for people who are vulnerable and lonely; they are referred to her by doctors and other professionals. The words 'vulnerable and lonely' repeat on a loop in Doris's head.

Natalie knows that Doris is a librarian and likens her own role to someone calling in at the library to read a book. Silent company, easing the frown lines, dissipating stress. 'We are both in the business of helping people,' she says.

Doris knows what she means about a face being transformed: she's seen people leaving the library looking younger than when they walked in.

'She wouldn't want to burden you – or anyone, for that matter. Understandably, her independence is extremely important to her. She talks about you a lot.'

'How utterly useless I am, I expect.' Doris tuts, exasperated by how little she knows about her own mother and how much this stranger does.

'No!' Natalie objects, surprised by Doris's reaction. 'Irene thinks a lot of you. I bet she's made up that you're here. She says you ring all the time and write to her.'

Doris hangs her head in shame then composes herself. 'What do you normally do when you visit?'

'Well, top up the bird feeders and note any newcomers. Your mum's good at identifying birds. The other month we saw a goldfinch. Irene was thrilled to bits because she's just read Donna Tartt's novel by the same name.'

'Donna Tartt – *The Goldfinch*, but that's fiction—'

'I make us a cup of tea, hold her hand, listen mainly. Help her find things again.'

In her mind, Doris had frozen Mother in time like the house, conveniently forgetting what time does to the mind and the body. 'She seemed to be coping so well last time I was here.'

'We cleaned for days to get ready for your visit. I'm not meant to but – well, I like your mum. I must do, given that I hate spiders and we must have wiped or hoovered up about thirty of the things! She got the mobile hairdresser round especially.'

Doris had thought that Irene's hair looked like it had been in rollers. 'I did wonder—'

132

'We're only meant to do the basics but your mum sometimes asks me to do the odd thing, like posting that letter to you or watering her pot.' Natalie smiles. 'She tries to keep on top of the housework, but with dementia you forget. I think of it like a moth, eating away at a woolly jumper.'

Doris tries to conceal shock, horror but it's written across her face like a placard.

'You knew about the dementia?'

Doris shakes her head.

Natalie shuffles in her seat but quickly regains momentum. 'The important thing is that you're here now. I expect you've been busy writing.'

'Writing?'

'Irene says you're a fantastic writer. She showed me some of your stories once when she was in one of her more amiable moods. They're excellent.'

'Thank you. Has she ever been aggressive with you?'

'Not Irene, but the dementia has. Mood swings are part of the course, unfortunately. I'd get mad if I lost things, large or small. Fighting old age and illness can be a good and a bad thing.'

The gratitude in Doris's eyes is heart-breaking.

'I'm sorry to hear about your husband walking out like that,' Natalie says. 'Your mum hopes you'll eventually think it was a blessing.'

'Why would she say that?'

'She said you were never interested in boys. John came as quite a shock.'

'We're divorced now,' Doris says, her cheeks burning.

'I'm on my second wife!' Natalie admits, laughing with her mouth wide open, exposing a large gold tooth at the back of her mouth.

'What on earth's that?' Doris says, startled.

'Irene's singing. I think it's "Amazing Grace". She loves to sing.'

'Music's good for the mood.' Doris says and smiles confidently. She looks at the painting of herself. She looks at it for a long time before she speaks. 'Did Mother tell you she painted that?' Doris can't stop looking at the painting of herself like she's never seen it before. 'Did you know that your thoughts and feelings can affect how you interpret something – a painting, for example? It's rather lovely, isn't it? She's quite pretty.'

Natalie nods. 'It's beautiful, Doris. I wish my mum had painted something like that for me!'

Doris's admiration and gratitude for Natalie overwhelms her for a moment. Through the lounge window, she watches her top up the bird feeder and then catches murmurs of her soft tones when she talks to Mother upstairs.

Before Natalie leaves, Doris does something extraordinary: she opens up her arms to hug her – a stranger. A perfect, selfless stranger. Without a hint of embarrassment, they embrace warmly. It's the second touch of physical contact Doris has had in almost a year.

'I have always depended on the kindness of strangers.'

'Tennessee Williams!' Irene shouts from her bedroom.

Before heading back to Shrewsbury, Doris fills up her mother's fridge and cupboards with food and makes the few dishes she is capable of cooking. She is worried about leaving her mother but the doctor and Natalie assure her that Irene will manage; she has before.

When it is time to leave, Doris feels upset. It's a peculiar feeling to have after years of dreading a four-minute telephone conversation. The whole time her mother has been here but now their relationship feels like a gift.

The yellow Beetle and the radio eat up the long motorway to take her home. By the time the sun is languishing in the sky, Doris realises she hasn't had a glass of wine in two days and she hasn't missed it a drop.

Chapter Twenty-Six

Dr Timpson says Doris doesn't have to be happy just because it's Christmas. It's taken the pressure off knowing that. He says he doesn't know how long she'll associate John's heartless exit with the Christmas season, that's up to her. Why he thinks she is so in control of her thoughts used to amuse her but, for the first time, she understands what he means.

She decides to speak to John so she can ask him the question that has haunted her for almost a year. Knocking at what was her front door is a peculiar experience, but it's quickly over when John opens the door to let her in. She follows him into the lounge, feeling like she's about to have a wisdom tooth extracted. His bed is in there, the old sofa and very little else.

'I need to know why you couldn't explain to me why you decided to leave me. I was in the kitchen, for God's sake, then I heard the door close. That was it. Our marriage over like that.'

John sits on the bed and puts his crossword to one side. 'If you're ready for the truth I'll tell you. Sit down.' He takes a deep breath. 'Doris, when you drink you forget what you say, what you do. I couldn't live with it any longer. The rare occasion you were awake to chat before sleep, you repeated yourself over and over.' He shakes his head. 'I missed you even though you were right beside me.'

Doris stares at him with a look of incredulity etched on her face. The pillow talk. It had got less and less. She thought it was because they'd run out of things to say to one another. She was the reason he left; the thought had never occurred to her.

John's face zooms in and out of focus. She clears her throat. This curveball has dried up her mouth.

'You know, some nights I just kept on talking, pretended you weren't snoring and dribbling right next to me, stinking of cheap wine. If you hadn't passed out all those nights when I was longing to talk, you'd know why I left you.'

'I was pregnant. Abersoch was meant to be… Then Lisa came with us. I didn't get the chance to tell you before…'

135

'Before what, Doris?' His eyes appraise her stomach. Her face. He is looking for an answer.

'I lost it.'

He nods like it isn't a surprise, scratches his stubble. His face looks tired and grey. Doris doesn't know what to say next. He has suffered. So has she.

'I'm sorry,' he says.

'Don't say that word. It's bollocks. She said it – Lisa—'

'I'm saying it, and I'm sorry.'

'Why? You're a dad, aren't you?'

'Yes and no. Lisa had a little boy. Jack.' A smile washes through his eyes. Doris is afraid he's going to cry. 'Look, Lisa took off when I started my chemo. She and Jack are up north, I think.'

'So, you met someone else?' She gestures upstairs.

For the first time, John laughs. 'Christ, no! She's only twenty. Lauren is my lodger. I'm not fit to work yet, let alone… It's some cash, just while I get myself sorted. I'll be back at work soon.'

'Soon?'

He avoids her gaze. 'Yeah, a month or two.'

Doris crouches down on her knees in front of John's bed, takes his hands in hers. 'I am sorry – I…'

'Don't.' He pulls his hands away. 'Your mum sent a couple of letters. They're in the top drawer there – one of the few you didn't destroy.'

She hangs her head in shame as she retrieves the letters that presumably ask her to contact Irene, that nag her about something she's failed to do. Their wedding rings are in there, too.

He watches with a steady gaze. 'She's always loved you.'

A photograph of a little boy in a blue-and-white Babygro takes central place on the chest of drawers. It is the only object to personalise the room.

'When did you last see her?' he asks.

'Don't.' This time her voice is firm. Whether he has cancer or not, the subject of her relationship with her mother is closed.

The word THANK YOU is still written across one wall in felt tip pen. It's not grown tired of watching her, like the eyes of T.J.Eckleburg.

'I passed my driving test,' she says weakly. 'First time. About the only good thing that came out of that trip to Abersoch.' She stands up, pulls her bag over her shoulder. 'I'd like to come back to undo the damage I did to the place.'

'Leave it be. It's just a house, a few walls.'

'It was our home!'

'Exactly. Was! Now it reflects how we ended up.'

'So that's it? We're done. You're going to stay in this grotty little hole and hope to get your strength back, cut me out of your life like we never existed? Is that the gist of it?'

'Yeah.'

'We both messed up, John. I don't want to forget eleven years of marriage. We loved each other once. I don't want you back – and I know you don't want me back either – but let's be friends. Look out for one another, that's all. Neither of us is exactly over-run with family or friends. I want to come back and clean the place up for me, as much as for you.'

She can tell he's tired and needs to sleep so before she leaves she draws the lounge curtains over the bare window ledge. She watches him climb under the ample covers, turn onto his right side, as he always has done. The familiar shape of him shoots pain up her vertebrae. His hair shows signs of regrowth like a field recently sown with seeds, tender shoots in lines.

She leaves his house without letting a single tear fall until she reads her mother's letters begging her to get in touch.

Chapter Twenty-Seven

Lisa's new address is 2a, Albert Way, Oswestry. Doris updates the library records with the sound of John's dejected voice in her ears: 'Up North, I think,' knowing Lisa has moved less than twenty miles away.

Lisa is taken aback when she opens the door to her flat with a towel in her hand. 'How did you find me?' Her pale face hardens like drying plaster.

Doris follows her into the living area. Jack is asleep on the carpet, which is home to an assortment of toys, a play mat and a squidgy book that looks like it might make an annoying squeak. Doris is tempted to pick up each one in turn and touch it. Does Jack have that almond smell? How does he feel in your arms? She pulls away her eyes. There is a sink full of washing up.

Lisa switches the radio off and waits for Doris to speak. She is immediately on guard and combative. An aggressive Lisa is new to Doris.

'John—' she stumbles, still shocked by the hostility emanating from her ex-best friend.

'John doesn't know where I am. Don't lie!' she yells. 'What are you doing here, Doris? If it's to make me feel bloody guilty for leaving John, you can piss off this minute. I told him to get his prostate checked months ago and he wouldn't.'

'Let me finish. John's in remission. He wants to see Jack.' The determined note in Doris's voice silences Lisa for a moment and her mouth sets into a hard line. 'I'm here because John's cancer has spread.'

'What the hell has that got to you with you, Doris? All I want is a little peace!' Lisa shakes her head. 'Since when do you give me orders?'

In a flash of anger, Doris imagines herself grabbing a fistful of Lisa's flaming hair, marching her across the room and throwing her into the car. She takes a deep breath before speaking. 'She wants peace! Poor old Lisa. Tired are we?' Her voice drops almost to a whisper. 'Imagine how tired John's feeling after months of chemo!'

Lisa closes her eyes. 'I won't be a carer again. Do you hear me? I won't. I want to live my own life and be a good mum to Jack.'

'If you can stop thinking about yourself for one moment, you might see your son needs a dad.'

Lisa looks at Doris like a wild cat. 'I doubt he'll want to see me.' Her voice is high and unnatural. 'I've not—'

'I haven't come here to gain anything. We've all been foolish, but I do know John wants to see his son. He's Jack's dad.' A thump from the upstairs flat startles them both, followed by a joyous laugh. 'What if he hasn't got long?'

'It was just meant to be a bit of fun! I admit my clock was ticking!' Lisa yanks out a tissue from the box on the table. 'I love Jack – he's the best thing that's ever happened to me. But John – it was only ever an affair.' She blows her nose. 'You didn't even reproach John or me when you came round. Why?'

Doris looks away, ashamed.

'Did you get my message?' Lisa asks. 'I was – am— I mean not about John, about us. Neither of us is right for John but you and me…'

'Stop it!' Doris gets out of her chair, her hands curled into fists.

Lisa moves towards Doris, afraid she might lash out but risking it anyway. 'I loved you,' she says in a low, resigned voice. 'But I knew you'd never—'

Doris moves to the door away from the tenderness in Lisa's eyes. 'None of that matters now. Only Jack. It's all gone. You've got responsibilities. What happened cost me my child. I've wished… It doesn't matter.' She shakes her head. 'Don't you see? Jack is all that matters and he needs a father.'

The tension in the room stirs Jack. There is a malicious pause. Lisa huffs then looks at her nails, anywhere but at Doris.

Doris remembers standing side by side on Abersoch beach, hurling pebbles hard out into the waves. In her mind, she throws one now containing a kernel of poison and spite. She stands and waits, smelling the sea air, tired of pussyfooting around with life. 'I'm not here to rake over the past. This is about Jack's future. And John.'

Lisa's mouth is about to open to fire abuse when Jack's eyes open and he makes a low, gurgling sound. It takes all Doris's strength not to bend down, scoop him up in her arms and run away with him. She plants her feet and focuses on the wall straight ahead like she was taught to do at school when giving a talk to the class. She takes a sharp intake of breath when Lisa goes to hold Jack and unbutton her blouse.

Lisa hears it and hesitates. 'I need to feed Jack before we go.'

It is the most beautiful thing Doris has ever seen and yet she winces and looks away.

'Will you be long?'

'Not usually.'

A lump rises in Doris's throat. 'I'll wait in my car outside. Grab what you need when you're ready.'

She doesn't get out of the car when she parks outside 42 Utkinton Street but, before Lisa gets out, she grips her arm. She can hear the sound of the waves. She doesn't let go for a while as the shape and form of Lisa morphs before her eyes. A carer. A fake friend. A woman she'd once desired. An adulteress. A single parent. Lisa. Forty-four. She knows there is nothing there that can resuscitate their friendship.

The light is flat when she feels a pang of grief, fleeting but real, and she moves her hand away. She feels its absence and then the sensation is gone. 'I'll pick you up in about an hour,' she says evenly.

Lisa nods and walks gingerly into the house like there isn't enough oxygen in the air. Doris thinks of John inside that vacant space, his mouth working its way into a smile at the sight of his utterly beautiful son, his eyes hurting at the sight, the sickness in him healing, pausing, mending, in a room without colour, white-washed.

They make her drink. Guzzle until her stomach is a well, so full it begins to pour over the top and trickle down Utkinton Street, a red rivulet, an S shape all the way to the corner shop and back. They still make her drink, sip it if she has to, faces at the bottom of the glass. She keeps drinking, swaying, and they are still watching. Then it is dark, the colour of a drinker's liver.

***

The worry of her phone ringing at the midnight hour reshapes her body into an exclamation mark on the double bed. A trace of spittle dribbles from her parted lips like an empty speech bubble. The discarded white sheet is writhed and twisted, freeing her previous captive hips like hostages. Erect, she grabs the phone, which is resting like a toad in the dark. She feels her heart pumping: fear, pert like a

140

fox's tail, thick with fur and scent. The artificial light from the phone casts flames onto the threadbare carpet, scooping out the hollows of her skull. The night bleeds out, slowly.

Natalie says, 'Don't panic, but your mum's been taken into hospital.'

A cat screeches. Doris steadies her hand on the staircase on her way downstairs. 'What's happened?'

Another fall. A blow to the head. Blood loss. Delirium. Asking for you.

Outside, mist is rising from the landscape. The grass is laced with dew, and leaves reach up from the grass and draw fleeting circles in the air. The petulant wind dispels the eternal circle to four corners as a filament of light stretches across the road like the Midas touch. The yellow Beetle pulls out onto the road and edges towards the motorway.

Chapter Twenty-Eight

'Mum won't move out of her house. I've tried everything and, if I'm honest, I wouldn't want to at her age,' Doris explains, as she makes Colleen and Andy a cup of tea.

'Can you get a live-in carer, perhaps?' asks Andy while sugaring his tea. He's made himself at home on Doris's new sofa, which makes Colleen smile. She loves his easy way with himself.

Doris recalls her mother's expression of arm-folded stubborn resilience during her last visit. 'She won't agree to it. While I was there she had a dizzy spell, came over all wobbly. It's only a matter of time before she falls again and seriously hurts herself. I couldn't live with myself if that happened and no one was—'

'Of course.' Colleen pats Doris's hand. 'What has the doctor said?'

'The aggressive outbursts are most likely down to dementia. I told him they'd started a few years ago, which he said sounded about right. God, I wish I'd known. And the dizziness is down to nothing specific. Could be not eating properly, loss of balance, old age generally.'

'I can tell you have something in mind,' Colleen says, as she carefully places her mug on a coaster.

'Would you cover for me at the library while I move in with Mother? I know Mr Morris would have to approve it, but I'm sure he'd be delighted to have you back full time. Just until – I mean, I don't know how long she's—'

Colleen nods immediately. 'I can do that, Doris, if that's what you want. It's such a shame when you've just bought your house.'

Doris shrugs. 'I'll rent it out. It'll still be here when I come back. I haven't been here long enough to feel too attached to it, except for the bathroom.'

'We'll visit you. How long does the journey take to Carlisle?' asks Andy, who loves a road trip.

'Avoiding a Friday, under three hours.'

Doris still looks tense, Colleen thinks. 'When do you want to go?'

'Tomorrow?'

She wants to leave early when most people are eating breakfast, warming up their bones after hours of being still. Leaving early feels like the only time to go. Any other time seems harder. She wants to leave before the world wakes up fully, when the sounds on the streets are muted, sleepy. Her bag is already packed and loaded in the boot of her car, so all she has to do is wash her face, dress, drive.

There's a service station at Lancaster that serves a decent breakfast, a welcome break from the long drive. It's in a new county. To stop before would be too tempting to turn around, go back. It's a plan that helps her go through the motions and make the final preparations before leaving. She places a one-pound coin in the piggy bank and closes her eyes, makes her prayer and then she puts Piggy in her handbag.

There's an enlarged heart in the space of her chest; it's waiting at the start line to a race. She is nearing the blocks to leaving Hollow Green and her life in Shrewsbury. There's no need to feel so scared. It's not like she will be homeless. Her bedroom is almost as she left it at Mother's place. There's a streetlight right outside her old bedroom window with an orange mouth that used to laugh at her small breasts and her mousey ways.

A glass of wine is tempting. A send-off. Justified. Almost, except for the early hour and the small matter of driving several hundred miles. Should she ring John? Lisa? Tina? Colleen? Goodbye over and over. Andy? The clock won't wipe its hours from its face. The spoon of John's body, the solidity of Andy's shoulders at the sink drying the dishes. Mother. A second home, for a time. Be a good daughter. She wishes she'd carved her initials into the wood panelling in the old school room before she left.

When the cloak of night is finally lifted, Doris dresses and locks up her house for one last time. Mr Russell Bromley's car is still in its spot. His bedroom curtains are closed. Does anyone notice she is leaving?

In one house the lights are on; steam spews from the utility room because the heating is on. The back door opens and a jerk of music, a DJ, escapes into the early morning. The neighbour is in a floral dressing gown and slippers, her hair half on her head, half down her back like a broken waterfall. Doris is tempted to call out hello or ring the doorbell, but instead she watches the woman put out the recycling. A cat crosses the road, arrogant, its tail a perfect exclamation mark.

The blind in Russell's kitchen is briskly moved upwards like a face yanked under a spotlight for an interrogation. He is wearing a white T-shirt, busy with a coffee machine. His elegant hand moves upwards to wave at Doris. She waves back, feeling lighter.

She was Andy's lemony heartache for a while, and then celibate in a perfect still-life of homemade dinners and plates washed in Fairy Liquid at Colleen's house. She was married, pregnant, deceived – for a while. All those months have gone away from her. She turns on the ignition. John lost his hair, his wedding ring, his wife of eleven years. Lisa Goodwood's name on the printout spewed out by the printer in the library, black print, small, loud.

Before she yields to the A5 and then the motorway, she swerves by the Darwin Library, Colleen and Andy's house, then John's. Dr Timpson will receive her thank-you note on Monday signed with a kiss. It's nine o'clock: a Saturday.

Doris catches sight of Lisa and John pushing Jack's pram towards John's house, its wheels shiny and silver with a black rim. He is holding a carrier bag – milk and bread, perhaps. The sun is on Lisa's flame-red hair and the back of her green coat, and there's a halo of light above John's shiny head. She could pull the car over and call out, say goodbye, but she is happy for them to have the last word.

Beyond the windscreen, the intense colours of the red, rosy and white sky and the freshness of new life on silver wheels mock and twist their beauty into a hollowing ache. She indicates right and makes her way towards the long road to Carlisle, to Mother, to begin again.

144

Rachel's Garden of Rooms by **Louise Worthington**
Finding answers in the most unexpected of places

Prologue

Your legs carry you to the familiar depths of the wood where the trees are so thick and dense, the sunlight barely finds its way to the earth. You pass like a shadow beneath the trees, merging with them, moving further and further away from Maple Cottage, from your home and through long grass and the gentle enemy of holly. Your footfall is the only terrible sound over twigs and fallen branches, over patches of ivy, monkshood and death mushroom. When you are satisfied you have found the best place, you begin to forage in amongst the chaos of trees and rotten wood, the fauna and the deadly.

Your wax jacket has ample pockets. You don't need to wear gloves for your task. It's perhaps late morning and you haven't eaten yet. Birds are startled and flee, shrieking and unsettling leaves as they burst through to open sky which is an indistinguishable stitched line of heaven where the eye of the sun watches, as if through a needle. Sand has been grafted out of the earth by badgers making sets and rabbits building a labyrinth of burrows. The sand looks red and tangy thrown in amongst the damp brown soil, armies of nettles and mossy stones. You screw your eyes up when you look at the leaves and berries in the soil-stained palm of your hand where the lines criss-cross like a path that some might say led you to this place. You can smell the spice of ferns, wildflowers and the unmistakable scent of a fox which stirs memories inside you of feathers. So many feathers. The memory draws you further into the world where woodpecker holes are the only eyes that watch you because no one knows you are making this dark pilgrimage.

Printed in Great Britain
by Amazon

39575779R00088